This Old House

A Gay Erotic Murder-Mystery

Joey Jenkinson

Copyright Joey Jenkinson 2017

1: The Journey

Their marriage had been a big mistake, right from the very start. Bren had never really loved him—perhaps she might have done, had there been children and were it not for the fact that every time they had had a row, it always ended up with her accusing Dave Rose of failing as a husband and prospective father by 'shooting blanks'.

Bren adored kids, and had spent so much of her life looking after other people's. Her mother, Millie Perkins, had had children like one shells peas—eight in ten years, like her parents before her—and was expecting her daughter and son-in-law to follow in the family tradition. For two years, sex had been anything but a pleasure—just one long cycle of charts, cold baths and thermometers, tablets, potions, consultations with complete strangers. Once, Bren had called Dave at the solicitor's office where he was one of the partners, and asked him to get home straight away because 'now was the moment'. The speakerphone had been left on, and Dave had headed straight for the toilet for a wank—the first time in months he had been permitted to shoot his load while not under extreme pressure. Not long after this, he had found himself a lover—Mick, the window-cleaner, who visited Dave's street each Tuesday afternoon, which by a stroke of luck was the day when Bren went shopping with her mother.

At thirty-two, Mick was two years younger than Dave, and like him a no-nonsense Yorkshireman—not particularly good-looking and a little on the tubby side, with a receding hairline—but he was *very* good at sex, and during their brief sessions assured Dave a better lay than he was getting from his wife. Each Tuesday lunchtime, Dave would make up some excuse as to why he had to nip out of the office. His colleagues had suspected that he was having an affair with a woman—they had heard Bren nagging at him every time she dropped in at the office, and were hardly surprised. Dave would arrive home half an hour before Mick was scheduled to turn up, and wait until he had finished the windows before nipping outside to announce that the kettle had boiled. Then it would be down with the shammy, off with their clothes, and a sweaty session on top of the bed in the spare room. Sometimes, if Dave needed to be back at the office to meet a client, it had been a mutual wank or a blow-job. But most of the time they had gone all the way, with Dave usually on the receiving end of a frequently rough ride but enjoying every minute of it—and always feeling slightly miserable afterwards because he would have loved nothing more than take their relationship to the next level by actually spending the night with Mick, at his place across town.

They had had sex away from the house just once, at the hospital, when on account of Dave's inability to get a hard-on—for no other reason than he had gotten into the habit of jerking off in the bathroom while getting ready for bed, anything rather than having to lie on top of Bren for five minutes and try and stay hard after he had finished, to make sure his load stayed where he had shot it—Bren had nagged him to go and see his doctor. And *what* a coincidence, finding Mick sitting in the waiting-room!

4

'An ingrowing toe-nail, at my age,' Mick had gruffed. 'I always thought that only old codgers got *them*!'

'That's nothing,' Dave had whispered to his friend. 'I've got to have a wank into this plastic pot, and I've got to do it here and hand it in while it's still fresh. I don't think I've ever felt so embarrassed in all my life! What happens if I can't shoot my load? What happens if I can't even get a hard-on? What am I going to tell the nurse?'

Mick had grinned at this. Dave was wasting his talents working in a stuffy solicitor's office. He should have been in films. He certainly had the looks: a lean, handsome face with deep-set brown eyes, long sexy lashes, a flashing smile which sent shivers down the spine. And *what* a physique, hidden under that designer suit! The first time Mick had seen Dave naked, he had whispered a silent prayer of thanks—that such a man could be interested in *him*!

'Follow me,' he had said. 'I got here too early. They told me it could be another hour before they call me in. Might as well have a little fun while I'm waiting!'

Dave had followed Mick along the corridor to the toilets. They had entered a cublicle, locked the door, and Mick had proceeded to snog his face off before unfastening his trousers and dropping these and his jocks about his ankles.

'Just what the doctor ordered,' he had smirked.

And *what* a lovely cock! Fine, thick and upstanding, a perky uncut seven-incher. Falling to his knees, Dave had wrapped his lips around the head and relished the salty tang

5

of sweat and pre-cum, before taking the whole appendage to the back of his throat. Mick had gently fucked his mouth for a good ten minutes before gently coaxing Dave to his feet and swinging him around to face the wall. Dave had never had sex in a public place before, and had been terrified of someone entering the next cubicle and hearing them. Grabbing his wrists, Mick had brought his hands up so that they had been flat against the tiles, and Dave had joked about him watching too many detective films as he had started to frisk him. Pulling down Dave's jogging pants, he had spread his fleshy, hairy cheeks wide, and poked the tip of his tongue inside his pucker. Mick had never done *this* sort of thing during their weekly sessions, and this deep probing had proved too much. Gritting his teeth, Dave had belted his load against the wall of the cubicle, and for a few seconds while returning to earth had forgotten why he had been at the hospital in the first place. Grabbing the plastic cup, he had scooped what he could retrieve of his jism from the wall. Then he had turned around and—because neither of them had expected this and therefore had no protection on them—he had finished off Mick with a few strong flicks of the wrist.

The irony, however, had not stopped there. Dave had handed his sample to the nurse, and a week later he and Bren had seen the consultant and been told that there was nothing wrong with either of them—they would just have to keep trying. Then, two weeks later, Bren's parents had had an almighty bust up, as a result of which her mother had schlepped up on the doorstep, unannounced.

'She's my mother,' Bren had said, just as annoyed to have Mrs. Perkins interrupting their routine as Dave had been. 'Besides, it'll only be for a day or two. They're always having rows and making up.'

The two days had become a week, then a month, until Dave had seriously considered committing matricide. It was not just that Maisie Perkins interfered in what they ate, what they should or should not watch on the television, where they should shop for their groceries—she had begun interfering in their 'breeding programme'. Maisie was disappointed that, after eight years of marriage, her daughter and son-in-law were still childless. And of course, in her eyes—given that large broods ran on Bren's side of the family but not on her husband's—Dave was the one to blame. Maisie had not only began advising the couple how to have sex—pronouncing one evening over dinner that Bren should lie still, on her back for half an hour once Dave had 'done his bit', so that it 'didn't trickle back out again'—she had advised him one morning, in front of the next door neighbour, to start keeping his underpants in the freezer, and to put on a fresh pair one hour before he and Bren went to bed, preferably during the afternoon when they were not too tired!

For Dave, this had been the last straw and he had savagely reminded Maisie Perkins—with a few well-placed expletives—that the term mother-in-law was an anagram of 'Hitler Woman', and that Maisie might in another age have been perfectly suited to running the camp at Buchenwald. Maisie's response to this had been to whack him across the

7

face. And here lay the final irony. Dave had called Mick, and arranged to meet him at the pub—and a friend of Maisie's had seen them kissing in Mick's car in what they had thought had been a discreet corner of the car-park, with Mick's stubby fingers wrapped around Dave's cock. Returning home, slightly the worse for wear but having spattered his load across the dashboard, Dave had found a note on the kitchen table. The friend had called Maisie, and she had gone back to her husband. Bren had gone with her.

This had been Monday. Yesterday, Friday, Dave had announced that he would be taking all of his annual leave at once. The other partners had grumbled about this—the firm were short-staffed—but had reluctantly agreed. Dave had friends in the West Country—good friends who would listen and understand. He would stay with them until he decided what to do about his marriage.

Dave now boarded the train at Leeds, removed his brown leather bomber jacket and tossed it into the rack above his seat, and settled down to read his newspaper.

'I'll write to Bren,' he told himself. 'I'll tell her we're finished. And if she wants a divorce now that she knows about Mick—well, I shan't stand in her way!'

Nick Quinn had got on to the train with a lousy headache, though it was now starting to wear off.

Last night had been spent crawling from one seedy city gay bar to the next. He had been hoping to find company, and though there had been several interested parties, each time somebody had approached him, Nick had muttered some lame excuse and moved on to the next bar. On his way home, he had asked himself if he had actually been *looking* for sex—or for reassurance that he could still pull a guy if he wanted to. Even the sexy young taxi-driver had given him the eye. And then, his best friend in times of need—his strong right hand—had deserted him once he had climbed into bed. Nick remembered getting hard as rock—fantasising about the taxi-driver—and starting the wank—but he had fallen asleep before reaching the finale.

Last night was meant to have been a celebration. After ten years of licking the supervisor's boots, Nick had finally been promoted to supervisor himself, and now he was taking a well-earned break, his first in three years. And how he needed this break—if only to get over Mark's death, something he had been trying to do for months without much success. Mark, who Nick's mother had often said had been a dead ringer for Montgomery Clift, whom she had idolised when young.

Nick had just turned thirty. He did not consider himself a particularly handsome man—while everyone else thought him drop-dead gorgeous. Six-feet tall and tipping the scales at 170 pounds he was possessed of facial features which would have driven a matinee idol insane with envy: hazel eyes, finely-sculptured cheekbones, a dimpled chin, a perfectly straight nose, and a shock of jet-black hair which he always kept immaculately groomed. Last year, Mark had proposed, and the civil ceremony had been arranged. Both sets of parents had approved of the union, and a reception had been booked and paid for at the Queen's Hotel.

9

Two weeks before the wedding, Mark had been killed in a car-crash. The other driver had failed a breath-test on the spot. Nick had been too distressed to attend the inquest, and the subsequent court hearing. The previous week, the same judge had given someone three years for possession of heroin, yet the shit who had killed the love of his life had received no more than a £500 fine and a six-month suspended sentence.

Nick's heart would never recover from the blow. He had boarded the train in Leeds, a little after ten. Just before eleven, as the train was leaving Doncaster, he glanced out of the window and observed that it had started snowing. This annoyed him, for he had not brought a top coat, or even a sweater, having expected the recent, unprecedented warm spell to continue.

'Easter bloody Saturday,' he cursed to himself. 'The Met men never said anything about snow...'

Trevor Kylesworthy had expected bad weather, though the forecasters had not predicted it. From personal experience, Easter was never to be trusted. Two years ago at this time of year, Paul had taken him to Paris for five days to celebrate his twenty-first birthday, and it had rained non-stop. Last Easter he had visited an aunt in Jersey, and it had rained then. As for snow—Trevor definitely did *not* expect snow in April! Good job then that he had dressed for winter, and had packed a spare sweater in his suitcase!

'Dartmoor must be pretty bleak when it snows,' he thought himself. 'Paul's village is miles from civilisation. I wonder if we'll be cut off? Could be exciting—knowing Paul, he'll have arranged another birthday I won't forget in a hurry...'

Trevor and Paul were ex-Londoners and had been lovers for four years. Paul was almost twenty years his senior, but this did not matter one jot—or that he was rich while Trevor was struggling to make ends meet, working as a locker-room attendant at his local gym. Age and money did not enter the equation. They had met in a bar—where else did gay men meet?—the muscular, loquacious hunk and the well-dressed businessman, an unusual relationship, initially. All evening, during their first date, Trevor had sported a hard-on. He rarely bothered with underwear and Paul had observed the outline of his swollen cock through the flimsy material of his chinos when he had taken him back to his house for a nightcap. Trevor had practically *begged* him to have sex with him, but the older man had been adamant: no sex on a first date. Paul had stayed over, but slept in the spare room—twice during the night he had gotten himself off, such had been his frustration. There had been no sex on the second date, either, or the third—they had been 'courting' for more than a month before Paul had introduced Trevor to his king-sized water-bed, and to the baby's arm hanging between his legs.

Gazing through the train window at the snowy scene starting to develop outside—and covering his lap with his magazine because thinking about Paul had given him a semi—Trevor envisaged the two of them, snowed in at the cottage which Paul hired for their little trysts when they had the urge to get away from city life. He saw them spending the entire long weekend in bed—breakfast, sex, lunch, sex, dinner, sex, and sex in between.

'Four whole days,' he mused to himself. 'Four days with Paul—and if we do get hemmed in and four days turns into four weeks or even four years, *I* won't be complaining!'

Johnny Rodrigues did not drink. He came from a long line of non-drinkers, virtually unheard of in his neck of the woods, and did not smoke either—or fool around with other men. In his whole life he had had just one lover, who also happened to be his confidante and soul-mate. Mike Brent—at thirty-seven, eight years his senior, and with whom he shared his life and a single heart.

Mike drank like a fish and swore like a trooper. Until giving up recently he had smoked like a chimney, and in his younger days had enjoyed the reputation of being a womaniser, though truthfully he had never really been attracted to the opposite sex. Then, he had been a rugby scrum-half, a member of a profession where hard-drinking and hard-shagging went with the territory. Mike had had several girlfriends, and he had bedded them all—but the best sex of all had always been with himself, alone in his bed, fantasising about his beefy team-mates who he knew would always be out of bounds. All this had changed when he had met Johnny—as excessively handsome as he was, and at six-two just a couple of inches shorter, muscular, *and* like himself hung like the proverbial donkey.

Johnny was Irish too, despite his name. His father was

Portuguese, and his mother had been a former seamstress from Killarney. According to her, true Irishmen were either ugly as sin, or devilishly handsome. Johnny belonged to the latter category, and never failed to turn heads. Yet he had never once even thought of straying from the 'marital' bed—he and Mike had been together for more than ten years. Mike had been there when Johnny had published his first crime novel, aged just nineteen and, in the wake of 'the scandal' when things had got tough with his rugby club, he had chosen to give up his career rather than his lover. Since then they had travelled the world in search of exotic locations for Johnny's books. They had visited India, China, Russia and Australia. Now, Johnny had decided that his new book would be set in...a North Devon caravan park!

'You and your bloody ideas,' Mike gruffed, as they settled into their seats on the train. 'I told you we should have waited until next month, when we get our driving licences back! But no, you were so bloody confident that it'd be blazing hot! Since when has April been anything but a washout?'

This was Mike, a big man with a voice soft and carefree as Erin dew—his big, steely blue eyes ablaze with mischievous anger, his jaw hard-set.

Johnny merely smiled. 'It won't last, Michael. 'Tis but a shower of snow, no more!'

Though travelling the world had relieved him of his Blarney—normally he spoke with just a slight accent, unless he lost his rag, which was very rare and almost always only when suffering from writer's block—Johnny's impersonation of the archetypal Irishman was a good one. Mike chuckled. Johnny had had more than his share of hard knocks. And he was not angry at him—just at the weather.

'I hope you're right, Johnny-Boy. Can you imagine what it's going to be like camping out knee-deep in snow—then trying to fuck each other all cramped up in a caravan, with the bloody thing rocking from side to side? The bloody thing will collapse, as sure as eggs are eggs!'

Mike could not understand why Johnny had wanted to actually *stay* in a caravan, rather than just use his imagination. He was loaded—they both were. When they had first met *he* had been the one earning all the money and he had invested wisely. Johnny's last book had been a smash, propelling him into the six-figure advance bracket. However, when he had challenged Johnny over their sleeping arrangements, he had been adamant—there was always the risk of that niggling little detail which the most astute reviewer might pick up on. Therefore they have to downgrade from their usual five-star hotel and rough it, even if just for a few days.

It had been warm, the previous day—Good Friday. They had put on shorts end eaten lunch on the lawn. Afterwards they had played tennis, and Johnny had won.

'Spring, at last,' Mike had proclaimed.

Today they were wearing denims and thermal socks, and chunky sweaters under their designer anoraks—and Mike was still cold. Johnny smiled and leaned his head on Mike's shoulder, mindless of the hostile stares from the middle-aged couple a few seats away.

'Could be fun,' he mused. 'I've never done the business in the caravan!'

The guard, clipping the Fellows' tickets, remarked that this sudden change in the weather was nothing to fret over. These freakish conditions often occurred well into May, especially in the West Country where this train was heading, but seldom amounted to much.

Even so, Kate felt cold. She buttoned her hand-knitted Aran cardigan up the neck—she too had anticipated good weather, and was wearing just a frilly white cotton blouse underneath—and leaned across the table to her husband.

'Tom,' she whispered. 'Don't look now, but have you seen those two young men ? They look so *normal*, yet each time they think nobody's looking, the blond one gives the other one a kiss—on the lips! I'm no prude, but it should never be allowed on public transport!'

Regardless of being told not to, Tom turned around to stare. He was ex-army, forty-seven and recently retired—a stocky, fearless individual with a booming voice and ebullient manner.

'Damned pansies,' he growled. 'National Service, that's what's needed nowadays. Makes men out of milk-sops. Never saw them behaving like that in Iraq!'

His prim and proper little spouse coloured at this.

'Tom, keep your voice down. They might hear. In fact, the fair-haired one's looking straight at us—and he's a lot bigger than you!'

The ex-colonel ignored the warning.

'Don't give a damn if they do. And it doesn't matter how big he is. In my experience his sort's rarely capable of knocking the skin off a rice-pudding. Now, how's about some more of that coffee?'

Kate opened the flask. The coffee was strong—it had a whole miniature bottle of rum in it, and plenty of brown sugar. She secretly hoped that the snow would not settle. Snow aggravated her sciatica—and she had forgotten to pack her pills.

The train pulled into Bristol Temple Meads, almost two hours behind schedule. Blizzard conditions prevailed, the guard announced over the tannoy, beyond Exeter.

Trevor Kylesworthy was pleased that he had packed a few woolens for the trip. He was twenty-three, muscular, healthy and fit through working out thrice weekly at the gym where he worked, but still susceptible to the cold. This morning he had put on a thermal vest under his sweater and even while travelling had kept his leather coat on. For once he was wearing briefs, which had been well-tented for half an houron account of the company he was enjoying. At one stage, he had taken advantage of the attendant passing with the refreshments trolley, blocking the other man's view, to shove his hand inside his denims and straighten out his cock so that the bulge might not be so prominent.

For this half-hour which has seen him sporting a raging boner, Trevor had not been able to stop glancing across at the man across the aisle. What a stunner! Around six-feet tall he estimated, and with the most gorgeous hazel

16

eyes he had ever seen! A shock of thick black hair, bushy but not too bushy eyebrows, and a slightly crooked Elvis smile which set his heart pounding like a drum.

And Nick Quinn was thinking to himself, returning the stare, 'This is the last thing I expected on this trip. But he's obviously interested—and so am I!'

Initially, they lapsed into a stilted conversation—about the weather. Both were well-spoken, though Trevor was not quite so posh—and he imagined as cultured—as the other man. Then Trevor excused himself to go to the toilet, and when he returned, there was no mistaking the diagonal bulge in his denims. Nick motioned for him to sit opposite him, and they resumed chatting about nothing in particular.

'I'm heading for Barnstaple, eventually,' Nick said.

'Eggesford,' came the response, the voice all sugar and spice. 'It's only a little place. Someone's meeting me there and driving me across to Okehampton. That's if we ever get there. I've missed two connections already—and you know what these cross-country services are like? It's also freezing on here. First they shut the buffet car because it's run out of just about everything, then the heating goes off!'

'Well,' Nick said, deciding to take the plunge and convinced that he was very definitely on the right track, even this early in their conversation. 'I can think of *one* way of keeping warm, if only for a little while!'

'Oh,' the other posed, well aware of what he was hinting at. 'And what precisely do you have in mind?'

Nick looked him in the eye, and ran the tip of his tongue around his thick, fleshy lips. He popped a button on

17

his shirt, and when Trevor observed the thick black bristles beneath his throat, he caught his breath. Nothing turned him on more than hirsute men.

'Give me a couple of minutes,' Nick said. 'Meet me outside the toilet—the next carriage but one.'

Trevor watched him stride along the aisle—nothing effete about this guy! He had brought rubbers but they were in his suitcase, so he hoped that the other man, whose name he still did not know, would be well prepared should they decide to go all the way. He reached up to the rack above him and pretended to get something out of his bag, and glanced up and down the carriage. The long-haired blond and the guy he assumed was his boyfriend were asleep, as were the older couple who until ten minutes ago had not shut up talking. He passed the toilet he had just used, and walked through the next carriage which was totally empty. The tall, matinee idol type was standing next to the open toilet door, and all but dragged him inside.

For several minutes, they devoured each other with hot, hungry kisses, crotches grinding, hearts hammering, zips almost at bursting point.

'Nick,' the man pronounced.

'Trevor,' he replied. 'Pleased to meet you! You must tell me if you come here often?'

Nick appreciated the joke. The preliminaries over and done with, Trevor unbuckled his denims. He was wearing pale blue briefs which already bore a damp patch from where his cock head had leaked its excitement. Kneeling down, Nick yanked Trevor's denims and briefs down to his ankles, and his thick, circumcised cock sprang free. As best he could, given that the train was swaying from side to side, Nick squatted and ran the flat of his tongue around the pink, swollen glans and enjoyed the salty tang of the other man's precum. Then the train lurched Trevor forwards, forcing Nick to swallow him whole, taking all seven inches to the back of his throat, until Trevor's nuts rested comfortably against his stubbled, dimpled chin and the tip of his nose was cushioned by the younger man's lush, fragrant pubes. Nick recognised the expensive brand of cologne—this boy had taste, *besides* tasting good!

The blow job did not last as long as Nick would have liked. Trevor was unused to having sex in iffy locations, and felt that—despite his excitement—he needed to get this over with in case someone had seen them entering the toilet, and alerted the guard. Therefore, when Nick attempted to take a breather, Trevor encouraged him suck harder until, bucking his hips, he let fly a torrent of sweet-tasting cream.

Nick stood up, and grinned, having swallowed the lot. 'Well, maybe it's a good job the buffet closed early. You don't get that kind of protein in British Rail sandwiches!'

Pulling up his denims but leaving his cock hanging out of his flies, semi-erect and still dripping, and suddenly no longer in a hurry, Trevor kissed Nick again, tasting his own sperm on his lips. Nick must have been in his hot blood because under his blouson he had on just a thin blue cotton shirt and, when Trevor unbuttoned this, nothing underneath other than a copious amount of dense, dark hair. Stooping,

Trevor suckled one nipple into a stiff little peak, then the other. This man was hot! Paul also had a hairy chest, but not as profoundly forested as this one! In next to no time, Trevor's cock was upstanding once more, something which had *never* happened, so soon, with Paul.

Nick lowered his trousers and boxers, and leaned unsteadily against the wall. His cock was not as large as Trevor had anticipated, though by no means small—almost as long and thick as his own, with a fleshy hood half-retracted over the shiny helmet. More than anything, Trevor wanted to feel this inside him, but the absence of a condom meant this would not be possible. Also, he did not fancy returning the compliment—blowing Nick—while the train was rocking from side to side, for fear he might gag.

'Shove your cock under my balls,' Trevor gently commanded. 'Fuck my scrotum...'

Nick chuckled at this. 'Well, *that's* a new one!'

Dropping his trousers to his knees this time, Trevor squirmed as Nick peeled back his foreskin, and slid his cock between his thighs and under his nuts. For Nick, this was almost as exquisite as actual penetration, and they kissed once more and allowed the train to rock them back and forth, Nick's cock-head cruising the damp tunnel formed by Trevor's low-hanging orbs and his warm, clenched together muscular thighs.

Winding his arms about Nick's waist, and with his own cock hard again and crushed against the older man's furry six-pack, Trevor dropped his hands and cupped them around the solid mounds of Nick's hairy rutting cheeks. The train stopped suddenly, almost throwing them off-balance, just as Nick let out a long, throaty growl and blew his stack.

They were brought back to reality by the guard's voice, bellowing down the sound-system. There was a blockage on the line ahead, he announced.

'Ha—but no longer a blockage in my cock,' Nick giggled, like a giddy schoolboy. 'Boy, I needed that! But look at you—ready to go again!'

Grabbing a handful of toilet paper, Trevor mopped the goo from around his balls and found himself saying, 'I guess it'll have to wait now—until we get on the next train!'

To which Nick responded, pulling up his trousers and grinning like a sheep, 'You mean you intend making the earth move *again*? I can't wait for that!'

Twenty minutes later, by now almost three hours behind schedule, the train pulled into Exeter St David's, where there was a mass exodus of irate and frustrated passengers attempting to catch connections, hire taxis, find buses, and use telephones because some of the mobile signals were down. Connections were running haywire, the buses had been called into the depots, taxis were few and far between, and two of the public payphones on the platform had been vandalised. Trevor managed to call Paul, but got only his answering machine.

The guard had fetched a tray of coffee from the kiosk on the platform, for those passengers still stuck on the train. He had spoken to the station manager who had assured him that transport would be laid on and that everyone would get to their destination with a minimum of fuss. A coach would be laid on to escort those bound for Plymouth and beyond, which left just eight Northbound passengers.

The guard approached Nick Quinn, who had stepped on to the platform to stretch his legs.

'They're putting on a minibus' he said. 'They reckon the roads aren't too bad heading up to Okehampton. Now, if you could make your way down to first class...'

Nick got back on to the train, informed Trevor what was happening, and they joined the others. Kate Fellows shivered and fretted. Her husband was making a nuisance of himself, threatening the guard and the railway company with a fate worse than death, should they be forced to spend the night here. Dave Rose chuckled at this. Tom's persistent ranting had helped take his mind of his marital problems and he was enjoying the spirit of the adventure. So what if they did have to stay here until morning? At least it was warmer in this carriage than it had been in the last one, and the seats had more leg room.

Opposite, the two Irishman sat huddled together, holding hands under their coats. The eighth occupant of the carriage, Janet Ellis, a thirty-something leonine redhead who Mike observed had worn a worried frown since boarding the train in Birmingham, surveyed the scene with interest. As a former psychiatric nurse, but now working for a private nursing company, she was used to harrowing situations. Opening her bag, she extracted a silver hip-flask and passed it to Kate.

'Cognac,' she smiled. 'They say it thins the blood, but it also warms the insides!'

The transport did not arrive until gone eleven. Eight stiff-limbed, weary and hungry passengers disembarked from the train and lumbered with their luggage over the footbridge and into the station foyer. The doors were wide open, and snow had drifted inside the building. The station manager personally escorted them to the minibus, which was parked in the forecourt. Its roof had a foot of snow on it. In the car-park, men trudged up and down with shovels.

The driver was a small, round-shouldered man of fifty, dressed in a donkey jacket and oilskin trousers. His name was Jack Gibbons and he spoke with a strong local accent. Nick asked him if the roads were as bad as the train guard had reported, and he shook his head.

'No, them be worse!'

'A bloody yokel,' Dave Rose muttered.

The nurse, squashed up against him on the back seat, suffused a smile. She reminded Dave of Gladys Emmanuel, the character in the Ronnie Barker comedy series he had loved watching as a child.

Tom Fellows, sitting in front of them, announced, 'I found a phone that was working. I called the hotel in Barnstaple and told them we'd be there by midnight.'

Jack Gibbons grinned back at him through the mirror. 'That'll be a miracle, zur. There be four stops before Barnstaple. Still, I can only do my best. Got four new tyres on the old jollopy. Reckon she'll plough through anything.'

The roads through the city had been cleared by the gritters and snow-ploughs, and it did not take them long to get onto the Barnstaple road. The snow, which had not stopped all day, now hit the windscreen in a solid sheet. The passengers, soon lulled into silence by the droning of the wipers, were wondering why in God's name this was happening to *them*.

After fifteen miles, the wipers gave up. Jack Gibbons wound down the window and drove for the next fifteen miles with his head hanging out of the window. It was impossible to distinguish between the narrow country road and the ditches on each side, while white-clad hedgerows and trees clustered together along the way like spectres. In next to no time, visibility was down to almost nil.

Kate Fellows' dentures rattled inside her mouth, on account of the icy blast whipping through the open window. She was also worried about her hair—she had only had it permed yesterday. Again, Janet was feeding her from the hip-flask.

'For goodness sake,' she snapped, shuddering herself, 'Are you trying to give us all pneumonia?'

The driver gritted his teeth. 'Could always swap places, missus, if you fancy driving through this lot.'

Janet opted not to say another word. She had felt on edge all day. New assignments always filled her with dread, and this bad start to the trip which was supposed to be the beginning of a new life was starting to convince her that something would go dreadfully wrong once more, like it had the last time with Agnes Pinder...

24

Janet was thinking about her last charge when the driver braked suddenly. Johnny Rodrigues, sitting behind him with a heavy rucksack on his lap, banged his head against the window and woke up. Jack Gibbons climbed out of the bus to examine what he had just hit. The front bumper was dented, and one of the headlights smashed.

'A bloody tree, smack in front of us in the middle of the bloody road. Too big to shift—looks like we'll have to turn around and take the slip-road!'

From within the vehicle, there was a babble of disapproval.

'I paid over the odds for that hotel. All that money wasted. Wonder if I claim it back on the insurance?'

'My friend's picking me up in Eggesford...'

'Bloody awful weather to be kipping in a caravan, Johnny-Boy! But I'm sure we'll think of some way of keeping warm...'

With difficulty, Gibbons managed a U-turn, but as he attempted the downhill slope, he cursed aloud as the engine stalled, then cut out altogether.

'We're stuck,' he announced.

'Stuck?' Tom Fellows echoed.

'Stuck,' Gibbons said again. 'Unless...'

He smiled to himself. The passengers were all ears.

'Unless what,' an Irish voice asked. 'What do you want us to do, get out and push?'

The passengers remained silent while Gibbons tried to re-start the engine. Cursing to himself, he flipped open the glove compartment and produced an Ordnance Survey map which he studied for several minutes before he realised he was holding it upside-down.

'It ought to be here, somewhere,' he said. 'I knows this area like the back of my hand. I was up here only a couple of weeks back....'

Trevor had had enough. The hurried sex on the train had been great, but since huddling next to Nick in the minibus to keep warm, he had been packing wood and would not have minded finding a guest-house and bedding down with him for the night. Paul need never know.

'Will you please tell us what we're going to do?' he asked, more politely than he would have liked.

'Yes, tell us do,' Mike gruffed.

'There's an empty old manor house. Can't be more than half a mile from here,' Gibbons said. 'They put it up for sale a few months back—the last owner neglected it, so it's going for a song. My brother was thinking of buying it.'

'Sounds like fun,' Johnny quipped.

The ex-colonel's wife was not amused. She had back-ache. The brandy had gone to her head because she had not eaten since lunchtime.

'Now I remember,' Gibbons said. 'We have to turn off at the bottom of the hill, and it's at the end of a lane. We can't do much more. The engine's kaput. If we sleep inside the bus it'll be like a deep-freezer in less than an hour.'

'An old manor house,' Johnny whispered to Mike. 'Could be used as a setting for the next book instead of the caravan site. I'll just have to upgrade the characters a class or two!'

'I'm not sleeping in some old barn,' Tom Fellows barked. 'I'd sooner take my chances with the bus!'

'Well,' Nick put in. 'I'm with the driver on this one. If this snow keeps up we shan't be able to see the bus come morning.'

'And we'll all die of fucking hypothermia if we stand here arguing,' Mike growled, stamping his feet and rocking the bus.

'Homosexual and foul-mouthed too,' Tom muttered to his wife. 'Two admirable qualities in a man.'

Before Mike could respond to this, Jack Gibbons leveled with them all. 'There's a tree down on the road behind us. Even if I get the bus started and we shift it, the road after that's a one-in-four. I'm going to find that house. You can please yourselves!'

Johnny was warming to the idea by the minute.

'The man's right, if the house isn't too far. We may find something to make a fire. I'ts goddam cold out here!'

This was the nearest the writer ever got to cursing himself, though his books oozed with expletives. His characters, he claimed, were pooled from the *hoi polloi* of the outside world—and there were few people out there who did *not* eff and peff.

He addressed the driver, 'This house—is it in good nick? I mean, it doesn't have the roof missing?'

Jack Gibbons hunched his shoulders. 'My brother's been to look at it. He said it was practically ready to move into—just needed some of the junk clearing out, and for the vendor to drop the price.'

'But wouldn't we be breaking the law?' Janet Ellis asked from the back of the bus.

'Who's going to be there to see us?' Gibbons asked.

'Who indeed,' Nick added. Not expecting any of this, he had left home without a top-coat. 'I don't mind telling you, I'm sitting here freezing my nuts off!'

'And I'm knackered,' Mike said.

And the driver was thinking to himself, 'I must have killed a bloody robin—stranded out here with two Mick homos and the weirdest bunch of characters I've ever clapped eyes on. Who could have wished for more?'

Then Kate Fellows broke her silence. 'Driver, just point us in the right direction and I'll lead the way. All this arguing—we could have been halfway there by now. It's only a couple of years ago—tell them, Tom—since I did the Lyke Wake Walk! Now that *was* an experience. Admittedly the weather wasn't as bad as this—'

'You didn't complete it,' her husband interrupted. 'And you had blisters on your feet for a week.'

'I managed twelve miles,' Kate said, proudly.

'There's one problem, though,' Trevor ventured. 'What are we going to do about food? I don't know about everyone else, but I've hardly eaten anything since breakfast.'

'Me neither,' Nick said. 'Well, I had a protein shake just before we got off the train...'

Trevor sniggered at this, and Mike smiled reassuringly, despite wanting to punch Tom in the nose. 'Me and Johnny have enough provisions in our rucksacks to feed a regiment for a week—well, for a weekend. The driver's right. We should find this house and at least try and get a good night's kip. Come morning, we'll find a farmer and ask him to get his tractor out, or something like that.'

'Mike and me have sleeping bags,' Johnny added. 'At least the old couple won't have to feel the cold. We don't mind roughing it, do we, Mike?

He was really looking forward to spending the night in some spooky old house, where things went bump in the night, and already his novelist's mind was going into overdrive. Mike only glared at him, as if to say, 'Why should I give up my comfortable arctic sleeping bag for a grousing old git who's done nothing but moan all day—and who called me a bloody pansy on the train and done nothing but make homophobic comments since?'

Tom glared at Johnny too, for calling him old. One by one, the passengers nodded their agreement.

It took them an hour to locate the house, by which time Tom had stopped grumbling. Dave Rose was beyond caring. Throughout the 'shall-we-shan't-we' debacle on the minibus he had kept his counsel. Now he was so cold, he was wishing he had stayed at home and opted to slug it out with his wife and mother-in-law—or better still, to slug it *in-and-out* with Mick, his window-cleaner lover!

Kate Fellows, supported by a chair of hands formed by Mike and Johnny, was thinking to herself, 'I'm going to be all aches and pains tomorrow. I do wish Tom hadn't kept nagging all the time we were packing the bags. Then maybe I wouldn't have forgotten my pills...'

Jack Gibbons had left the minibus in the middle of the road—he had no choice—and he was dreading having to dig it out in the morning.

Janet Ellis was experiencing tormented thoughts, remembering an old silent film she had once watched on one of the cable channels—about two children who had wandered off into the snow, fallen into a drift, and not been found until the following Spring when the thaws had come.

Nick and Trevor, trudging knee-deep through the snow and holding hands, were in their element—since meeting on the train, neither had thought for one moment about anything other than the next time they would be having sex.

'There's going to be a next time, of that I have no doubt,' Trevor was thinking to himself.

And Nick was thinking, 'This guy's got me feeling so horny—and he *so* reminds me of Mark, if I had half the chance I'd fuck him right here, right now in the snow while everybody's watching."

2: The House

Nick saw it first. The stone facade looked imposing, seen through the sheet of blinding snow, and the property itself appeared a good deal smaller than he assumed a country manor house should. The tall, wrought-iron gates surmounted on either side by snow-capped obelisks, reminded him of the entrance to a sanitorium—of the type seen in old black-and-white movies. All that was missing were ravens on the roof. Had the weather been more clement, and he less eager to get past them and hopefully find shelter, Nick might have observed the family crest in the middle of the railings.

He turned to Jack Gibbons. 'How do you know the place is empty? What if there's somebody inside—some old matron in a tweed suit, brandishing a shotgun?'

'If it's occupied, all the better for us,' Gibbons shot back. 'I wouldn't bank on it, though. Like I said, this house has stood empty for twelve months or more.'

The little party battled on, defying the arrows of snow which were rapidly turning into sleet, bodies bent double against the fierce wind. The gates had been left open—it was as if the old house had been expecting company. The journey from here to the building alone seemed to take an eternity, the drifts on either side of the path man-deep in parts. Mike Brent and Johnny Rodrigues, despite their size and strength, found the going tough, as they stumbled to where they assumed the front door should have been.

'Anybody that wants to live in a God-forsaken hole like this needs their head examining!' Mike exclaimed.

31

They located the studded oak door, and Mike would have attempted to kick it in, had not Dave Rose yelled something about burglar alarms and breaking and entering.

'Burglar alarms, my left tit,' he growled. 'Hey, Johnny-Boy. Have you got your torch handy?'

There was more fumbling, stumbling and cursing before the strong beam of Johnny's flashlight picked out a window to the right of the door. Unable to find anything better on account of the snow, Mike removed one of his size 11 boots and used it to smash the glass. Reaching inside, he located the catch and the window swung open. Moments later, he helped Johnny through the aperture, not forgetting to give his rump a friendly squeeze.

Tom Fellows stamped his feet. Though he would never have admitted it, he had always been afraid of the dark and the shadows cast by this old house unnerved him almost as much as this enforced company of odd-bods. He wanted to stick his head through the window and tell the big Irishman to get a move on, but there was an even bigger Irishman standing behind him and, close up, he did not like the look of Mike Brent at all. He had insulted him on the train when there had been no repercussions to fear, and again more recently—now he was going to spend the night with him in a mysterious house in the middle of nowhere.

Mike made an attempt to follow Johnny through the window—only to gash his knee on a slither of glass and let rip some of the foulest language some of the others had ever heard. Then after ten minutes, Johnny emerged from around the back of the house.

'I found a spade,' he announced, a broad grin spreading across his flushed, handsome face. 'I busted the lock off the back door. The snow's not too bad around there.'

The party now found themselves having to struggle through a shrubbery—the path down the side of the house was piled high with rubbish and boxes.

'Welcome to the happy home,' Johnny panted, as they reached the door.

Dave turned to the nurse—he was carrying her suitcase as well as his own, while she assisted a now visibly shaking Kate.

'The happy home's where he ought to be,' he muttered. 'Stupid Irish twit!'

The company crossed the threshold, and Mike glared at Dave, having heard what he had just said about Johnny. Was this how it was going to be all night—insults flying all over the place? Instead of saying something back, he exacted his revenge on the door—slamming it so hard that the house seemed to shake on its foundations.

Janet glanced about her, anxious, taking in what little she could see from the waving beam of Johnny's flashlight.

'I don't like this one bit,' she said.

'Me neither,' Mike returned, the wind whipping his fair hair about his face. 'But it's like the driver said, fair shelter for the night. Come morning, we'll all be on our way. There'll be some town or village nearby—has to be!'

Janet was hoping so. It seemed an eternity since they had left Exeter. But she had seen the fallen tree, and readily assumed that the slip-road would be blocked for some time.

If only it would stop snowing, then maybe they would get back to the main road, wherever this was...

'There was another house,' Trevor chimed in, from somewhere within the room. 'Or maybe it was a cottage. We passed it just before the bus broke down. I didn't notice any lights on, though. Oh!'

He recoiled, as the beam from Johnny's light caught him in the face. Johnny apologised. He had an attractive smile, Trevor thought. Then he realised that he was still holding Nick's hand, and had been for most of the time since leaving the minibus.

They were standing in an old scullery, judging by the assortment of old-world utensils: copper pans, earthenware pots and bowls, an old washboard and a busted peggy-tub, a butter-churn, a tea-chest filled with rusty tools, and a broken mangle.

Trevor picked up a copper pan. 'Well, at least there's no shortage of things to use if we want a brew!'

Nick let go of his hand, and crossed to the sink. 'The water's still on, too!'

He twisted the tap, and dirty brown liquid cascaded into the filthy enamel sink. After a moment, it ran clear.

'I suppose it'd be asking too much for the electricity to still be connected,' Tom Fellows bellowed.

They tried the switches—it was not.

Nick watched the water gurgle down the plug-hole and said, 'One night's about all I could stand in this dump. I'd have sooner bedded down on the train. I don't think I've ever felt so cold in my life."

34

And Tom was thinking to himself, 'That's your own fault. You should have put more clothes on.'

Jack Gibbons was rummaging through cupboards. Suddenly he held up a box of candles.

'Now all we do is find a room to sleep in where there's no bugs and things,' he chuckled.

He doled out the candles, like a teacher handing out exercise books—one for each person in the room, and shoved the remainder into the pocket of his donkey jacket.

'I remembers coming to this place once before, when I was a kid,' he said. 'It was full of junk, then. Who knows, we might find a few sticks of furniture to make a fire.'

Nick nudged Trevor and whispered in his ear, 'Why does he keep saying *I remembers* and *I knows*? Don't they teach them elocution in these parts?'

Trevor checked to see if anyone was looking, and grabbed a handful.

'All I *knows* is that I *feels* randy as hell,' he mocked.

'Me too,' Nick replied. 'But somehow I don't think there's going to be much chance of us getting our end away in this place…'

The scullery led into a large, empty room. Johnny entered first, brandishing his torch in front of him like a weapon. He started as a mouse—or was it a rat?—ran over his foot and scurried into a corner. Shuddering, he all but ran across this room and into the next one. He had always been afraid of rats. The others followed, hot wax from the flickering candles scorching their fingers. Trevor tightened his grip on Nick's hand.

35

The next room contained a large open hearth with an old-fashioned mantelpiece. A huge bay window took up one wall. Hanging from the other walls, festooned with cobwebs, were half a dozen prints—Johnny doubted these could have been worth much, otherwise they would not still be here. There were a few items of furniture: an oblong dining table, two chairs which has seen better days, two armchairs a sofa with most of the stuffing hanging out, and a commode. Stacked under the window was a pile of broken chairs. Johnny pointed to these with the beam of the torch.

'At least there's no shortage of firewood,' Dave observed. 'I shouldn't think the vendors would mind us burning this lot!'

'They won't have much choice,' Tom said. 'It's either that or we freeze to death.'

He flopped into one of the armchairs, raising a cloud of dust which made him splutter. His wife had been laid on to the sofa—Janet was on her knees, chafing Kate's hands. Trevor sorted out several pieces of broken chairs and passed them to Nick, who stacked them in the grate. Dave wrung his hands together and cracked his knuckles.

'Maybe we should explore the rest of the house,' he suggested. 'There might be some beds.'

The ex-colonel grunted at this, 'Hmph. I'm staying down here if we can get a fire going.'

Mike was in the other arm chair. He had rolled up the leg of his denims and was examining his cut knee, certain that it needed a stitch.

'You can please yourself,' he told Tom. 'Christ, there's still a chunk of glass in this...'

'Then hang on to your agony for a minute or two,' Janet said. 'Poking around will only make matters worse!'

Like a child, the big man obeyed. For the first time, courtesy of the candle perched on the edge of the dining table next to her, and the fact that she had removed her woolen hat, he observed that she was a red-head and rather brassy-looking—exactly the type he had preferred in pre-Johnny days before he had discovered the more rewarding delights of man-to-man sex.

Meanwhile, David Rose ventured the two flights of dusty, creaking stairs to the next level of the house, Nick and Johnny close on his heels. The upstairs landing was disgusting—it reeked of cats' urine and there were mouse-droppings everywhere, and the remains of a dead rat which Dave kicked into a corner. Johnny, separated from Mike, felt nervous and unsure of himself with these two, despite his size.

And Dave was thinking to himself as he brushed the dust off his bomber jacket with the back of his hand, 'This Irish guy—he's quite cute, but there's something about the other one, Nick, that both turns me on and freaks me out.'

There were seven bedrooms in all, two of which contained beds which looked like they might have boasted a life of their own. Each room had a fireplace, a smaller version of the one downstairs. There were also two bathrooms: one was full of junk. In one of the cupboards, Nick discovered a large pile of ex-Army blankets—a dozen of them, all neatly wrapped in plastic! He carried these downstairs.

Dave shivered. 'I don't suppose anyone's even thought about food. I'm famished.'

'Like Mike said, there's food a-plenty in our rucksacks,' Johnny told him. 'God forbid we should need to stay here longer than tonight. We don't mind sharing at all. We've also got a small camping stove and a couple of canisters that we brought along in the event of an emergency. It'll be safer than cooking on the fire, though God knows it'll take some organising, feeding nine of us. We'll have to do sittings. It'll be like being back at school!'

Dave indicated the two rooms which contained beds. 'At least the women will be comfortable, that's if the mattresses aren't crawling with fleas. I can make do with a couple of those blankets and sleeping in my coat.'

He had the sudden urge to get away from this man—not that he found Johnny disagreeable company to be around—quite the reverse, the gentle lilt and not to mention the flashing smile was starting to give him wood—but Johnny had a short-tempered boyfriend even bigger than he was. He descended the stairs to rejoin the others, while Johnny used the bathroom.

Downstairs, Nick had got a fire blazing, and Trevor was handing out mugs of coffee—obviously the fire was far more efficient than Johnny and Mike's camping stove. Mike had opened a packet of biscuits and was rationing them out. Kate Fellows was still on the sofa, dragged within scorching distance of the hearth. Wrapped up in one of the blankets, Dave thought she resembled an Egyptian mummy. Her husband had stopped complaining, for now.

Kate smiled up at Dave. 'Did you find anything up there, dear? I hope there aren't any ghosts!'

In her own way, Mrs. Fellows was having fun!

'Just a couple of beds and lots of mouse-muck,' he replied. 'I think you'll be better off sleeping down here, near the fire.'

'Me too,' the nurse put in. 'I feel safer down here where there's a few of us.'

'Okay, so Johnny and me will take one of the beds, and our sleeping bags are there for whoever wants them,' Mike said. Then he glanced at Nick and Trevor, and winked. 'Guess you guys will be wanting the other bed?'

Nick shrugged his shoulders, looked at the younger man and feigned indifference. 'I'm so whacked, I could sleep standing up. I hope you don't snore?'

Trevor chuckled at this, collected a newspaper and an armful of wood from the broken chairs, and followed Nick up the stairs.

They remained patient until Trevor had smashed the wood into smaller pieces and stacked them in the grate, and Nick had rolled up the newspaper and set the fire going. The room was small, and did not take long to get warm, though the mattress was damp and smelled of must. Nick spread one of the blankets on top of it, then took Trevor by the hand and coaxed him to stand in front of the fire.

'You're a beautiful guy,' he murmured. 'I've never been

one for having sex on an impulse, as happened on the train. You must have thought I was a real slut!'

'I never thought anything of the kind,' Trevor replied. 'It was *me* who came back from the toilet with a boner, remember!'

Nick smiled, and his voice almost sounded as if he was going to burst into tears. 'I took just one look at you and saw how truly beautiful you were. You remind me of someone I once knew...'

Trevor detected the sadness in his voice, and decided not to press for details. They kissed, at first just a brushing of lips, then passionately, so much so that they eventually had to move away from each other to catch their breath. The sex on the train had been great, but hurried. Now, despite the tawdry surroundings, they had all night —Trevor had wedged a chair leg behind the door to prevent anyone from wandering in during the night.

'You scrub up well yourself,' he found himself saying.

Taking his time he unbuttoned Nick's shirt, gradually exposing the sooty expanse of bristles which covered his top half, from just below the hollow of his throat down to the deep indentation of his navel. Nick removed the shirt himself, and flung it onto the bed. Raising one slightly muscular arm and then the other, he exposed his pits, equally dense. Trevor nuzzled and licked them, one by one, turning them into soggy quagmires.

'I don't think I've felt this horny in my life…'

Nick chuckled at this and kicked off his shoes, but kept his socks on. Turning his back on Trevor, he removed his denims and boxers, and stood still for a moment to enable the other man to enjoy the view. The broad back and shoulders were perfectly smooth and lightly tanned, as were the rounded cheeks of his buttocks, his long legs pleasantly hirsute. Then he swiveled around, placed his hands on his hips, and Trevor's heart skipped a beat. Nick's cock was so hard that it was almost touching his abs, the foreskin drawn tightly back over the glistening head. Trevor sank to his knees, and cupped Nick's scrotum in one hand while applying a spit lick around the ridge of this beautiful appendage. Parting his lips, he took in the tip, drawing hard, savouring the salty-sweet taste of precum. For a few minutes, Nick gently made love to his mouth. Then, reaching down, he urged Trevor to his feet.

'You'd better get your kit off,' he mused. 'I don't want the baby to burp just yet—not until I've seen you in all your naked glory!'

Trevor stood back and removed his pullover, then the thermal top he had on underneath, then his vest.

'More skins than an onion,' Nick quipped, skinning his log back and forth as his nuts rose expectantly into their now-tight bristly pouch. 'I don't know about you, but I feel like coming a bucket-load!'

Trevor kicked off his shoes and stepped out of his denims, leaving on his socks and bulging pale blue briefs. Squatting on his haunches, Nick pressed his lips against the flimsy material, then traced the full diagonal length of the stiffening cock within, his nostrils keening to the heady aroma of hunk on heat. Drawing these down very slowly he

41

exposed Trevor's thick log inch by inch, taking time to savour the neatly-trimmed dusky pubes, until finally the object of his attention sprang free, its flared purple head bobbing up and down several times before settling at a right angle to his hairless abs. Nick licked his balls, sucking them into his mouth one at a time, then slurped underneath his scrotum, tasting where he had exploded, earlier. Then he ploughed down on Trevor's cock, taking all seven inches to the back of his gullet. Trevor gritted his teeth, and ran his fingers through the other man's thick, black hair and desperately tried to hang on to his wad.

Eventually, when all seemed lost, Nick regurgitated Trevor's manhood and rose to his feet. They kissed again and held each other tightly, Nick's hard-on wedged under Trevor's scrotum, as had happened on the train. Then Nick broke away from him, reached into the pocket of his discarded denims, and fell backwards on to the bed, arms and legs akimbo, his cock flattened and leaking against his abs. He opened his hands. In the palm of one was a pack of rubbers, in the other a tiny sachet of lube.

'Fuck me,' he murmured. 'Please...and you don't have to be gentle if you don't want to!'

Trevor did not need telling twice, though he had hoped that it might have been the other way round. Tearing the foil packet open, he rolled the condom the full length of his cock and, climbing onto the bed, eased himself between Nick's thighs, hooking one foot over each shoulder. Nick's anal trench was as pleasantly hairy as the rest of him, and Trevor wanted to plunge his face between those cakes, and pig out until the moon turned green. Instead, he inserted two well-lubed fingers, worked these around for a few minutes and, satisfied that Nick was ready for the real thing, sailed home in one thrust. Nick's groans of pleasure were such that it echoed throughout the old house.

The fuck lasted much longer than either had expected, perhaps on account of them both having offloaded just hours before. Nick lay back, taking his punishment like a man, the veins in his own cock bulging almost to bursting point as Trevor pistoned in and out of him, sometimes withdrawing completely if he thought he was getting close, then pausing for a moment before slamming back inside. Occasionally, he slowed down so that they could kiss. Then, when he was almost there, Trevor wound his fingers around Nick's cock, and despite his own frenetic thrusting masturbated him so tenderly that the urge to come was almost unbearable. Clenching his sphincter tightly around Trevor's overcharged weapon and all but cutting off the blood supply, Nick bucked upwards off the mattress and let rip—several spurts of jism speared across his abs and chest, the first forming a puddle in the hollow of his throat. With immaculate control, Trevor kept thrusting—until he was sure that the other man had nothing left to shoot. Withdrawing his cock, he lost the rubber, and a few strokes later and with more noise than he probably should have made, zigzagged his load across Nick's chest.

'Wow,' the older man panted, as Trevor rolled onto his back, his cock still leaking like a tap. 'That really *was* worth waiting for!'

43

Downstairs, Kate Fellows lay fast asleep on the sofa, while her husband snored, his mouth wide open, in the armchair. Johnny and Mike were sipping their third mug of coffee and anticipating the fun they would have when they went upstairs. Jack Gibbons was nowhere to be seen.

'He said he was going down into the cellar to see if there was any coal for the fire,' Janet said. 'Rather him than me. I've only been as far as the door, and that was far enough.'

'He told me the nearest village was twelve miles away,' Mike put in. 'That's going to be some serious walking...'

'Twelve miles? Johnny exclaimed.

'Hang on to your shirt, Johnny-Boy,' Mike went on. 'I was going to add that he says there's a telephone box, half a mile down the road from the end of the drive. What I can't understand is why we can't get signals on our mobiles. Mine was okay when we were on the train.'

'Mine too,' Janet replied. 'I guess the mast must have been affected by the adverse weather conditions. Something

like that. But there's got be a farm nearby. I mean, isn't Devon supposed to be nothing but farms? I think we should get up early and go off in different directions until we find help. Don't you agree?'

Johnny and Mike nodded—Mike had already volunteered to help the driver dig out the minibus. A few minutes later, bidding the nurse goodnight they gathered up what remained of the broken chairs and climbed the stairs to their room. Mike chuckled as they passed the door of the room next to theirs.

'Sounds like somebody's having fun,' he whispered. 'Don't know about you, Johnny-Boy, but I'm feeling as horny as a three-peckered billy-goat!'

Janet Ellis was too tired to think any more. She should have been happy. She had left the Midlands for good, but her bad dreams and anxieties would follow her wherever she went. She knew that, weary as she was, she would almost certainly be in for another interminable, sleepless night.

Johnny—the pretty Irishman—had loaned her his sleeping bag. It had been a kind gesture, of which there had been few of late. The age of chivalry was not dead. Balancing her candle on the window-sill, Janet studied her reflection in the darkened glass as she dragged the brush through her long, red hair, and cursed to herself.

'Christ, all this business has made me start to look like an old wreck. I've got bags under my eyes—more wrinkles than the prematurely-aged biddy on the sofa. I'm thirty-nine and I look like I've been dragged to hell and back!'

Moving away from the window, she put away her brush. Johnny's sleeping bag bore the all-too-familiar scent of intense masculinity. Johnny may have 'batted for the other team', but there was nothing remotely effete about him—about either of them—and as she snuggled into the soft fabric she felt more secure than she had for some time, safe from the ghosts of her past.

'Not all men are shits,' she said to herself.

She closed her eyes, hoping for the sleep which might not come for hours, and her thoughts came flooding back.

'The old lady—it *wasn't* my fault. They knew I wasn't in the house when it happened...'

Then her mood suddenly changed to one of unanticipated optimism.

'It's going to be different from now on. My name's been cleared. If they say anything now it'll be slander. I'll sue—like I should have done before!'

Schoolboy giggles pervaded the silence, coming from upstairs. Johnny and Mike, she guessed—or the other two. Then she drifted off into a deep and dreamless sleep.

In their room, Mike squatted precariously over Johnny's face—both were naked, and his lover was giving him the rimming of a lifetime. Mike squirmed as his balls rubbed against Johnny's whiskers. Absolutely *no one* ate rump like Johnny, and Mike had often wondered who had taught him to do it so inordinately well, and guessed he must have picked up a few pointers from the Eastern European porno films he liked to watch. When they had met, though *he* had been around the block a few times—but only with women, several of whom *had* been into rimming, which he had considered odd, if not perverse, though he had never complained—Johnny had been a virgin, nineteen and green as grass. Well, he had made up for lost time since then!

Spreading Mike's massive, slightly furry alabaster cheeks, Johnny's expert tongue explored every which way, encircling the hard rim of Mike's sphincter, every now and then probing inside and getting him to open up so wide, it was no small wonder he could not see his tonsils. Sometimes, when Johnny did this, such was the intense pleasure that Mike had to beg him to stop to prevent him from shooting too soon—or from passing out, whichever came first.

Mike steadied himself by spreading the fingers of both hands across Johnny's raised knees. Half an hour ago, this room had been like an ice-box, but Mike had lit a fire, which might not have been necessary, given the amount of heat they appeared to be generating right now—the hairy mounds of Johnny's pecs were already sweat-lacquered and slippery, and they were still only halfway through the preliminaries!

'I wonder who's doing who, next door?' Johnny asked, between noisy slurps. 'Do you reckon they both like it rough? Posh boys invariably do.'

'And how would *you* know that, Johnny-Boy?' Mike posed. 'Unless there's something you're not telling me?'

'I was thinking about some of the books I've read,' Johnny returned, outstretching his legs. 'You know, *Brideshead* and all that stuff...'

'I've read that too,' Mike put in impatiently. 'To me they just seemed like a couple of sissies. Who wants to be fucked by a guy who takes a teddy-bear to bed with him? And that skinny guy in the film you made me watch—if you ask me, a good fuck would have killed him. God, that feels *so* good. You're really hitting the spot, Johnny-Boy!'

The candle flickered and played tricks on Johnny's long, hirsute form spreadeagled beneath him, making his already big uncut cock look even bigger as it lay flattened against his abs, the tip reaching past his navel, a tiny droplet leaking from the smiling slit. Leaning forwards, Mike kissed this away and Johnny shuddered. Johnny was the only man he had ever had sex with, or even wanted to. In this respect he too had been a virgin when they had met.

'All I'm interested in is who's going to be doing who, here,' he murmured. 'God, I don't half love you!'

Leaning further forwards he opened wide and took all eight inches to the back of his gullet, until his chin was buried in Johnny's pubes. Johnny raised his knees again so that Mike could work the fingers of one hand between his cheeks and strum his pucker. For a moment he lay off feasting, and bent Mike's massive weapon backwards between his thighs, working back the fleshy foreskin so that he could take the fat, vee-shaped head into his mouth. For several minutes they kept this up, pausing only when the noises next door intensified, then stopped.

'Sounds like another load's been shot,' Mike mused.

'And you shouldn't talk with your mouth full,' Johnny got out. 'It's rude!'

Regurgitating Johnny's cock, and retrieving his own to prevent it from going all the way down Johnny's gullet and bringing the show to a premature finale, Mike sat up, stretched and flexed his melon-sized biceps. Turning around, he knelt across Johnny's thighs so that they were facing, and slowly lowered himself onto his iron-hard cock.

The intense rimming meant that there was no need for lubrication, and because they had only ever been intimate with each another, condoms had never entered the equation.

Mike gave a little moan as the head of Johnny's cock slid inside his chute, and Johnny reached forwards to begin stroking his own. For years, Mike Brent's cock had been the talk of the rugby team. The other players had ribbed him about it in the locker-room, declaring how it was as big, soft, as most of theirs were erect. Once, after a match, each of his team-mates had slammed a ten-pound note down on the bench, to be donated to charity, but only if Mike satisfied their curiosity by getting hard so that they would know if the rumour about him being hung like a horse—according to the captain's wife—was true. Mike had obliged, 'turned on' by their dirty talk about wet pussies and soapy tit-wanks, and the captain had produced a tape-measure. Since that day, and until giving up the game, Mike had borne the nickname 'Ten-Inch Brent'.

Now, this sturdy ten-incher slapped back and forth as Johnny got into his stride, thrusting upwards and hitting his prostate while Mike leaned forwards and gripped his shoulders and hoped that the creaking bed would not collapse under the strain of 370 pounds of rutting beefcake.

Johnny reached up to tweak Mike's nipples, his sign that he was approaching blast off. Grabbing his cock with both hands Mike whacked off like a man possessed, and as Johnny grunted his load deep inside his bowels, Mike threw back his head, and blasted the carpeted torso beneath him with half a dozen piping, creamy streamers.

49

'I love you too, Mikey,' Johnny panted, dipping a forefinger into Mike's steaming, copious load and reaching up to trace a spermy heart across his lover's broad, perfectly smooth chest. 'Always have, always will!'

Jack Gibbons had slept like a log, on the floor in his donkey jacket and oilskins, and with the blanket covering his head. If there were things creeping around the house at night, he did not want to see them.

Still under the blanket, he squinted at the luminous dial of his wristwatch. The bigger of the two big Irishmen had promised to help him dig out the bus. They had agreed nine, and it was now five minutes past ten! He would have left without him! Then Jack reminded himself that the other man was a stranger to these parts, and as such would probably get lost before reaching the end of the drive, let alone before locating the telephone box. Pulling the blanket away from his face, he saw that it was still dark.

'Now, there's a funny thing...'

He removed his watch, shook it, and saw that the second-hand was still moving. Then he got up and crossed the room, and almost tripped over something in front of the hearth—the nurse, snoring her head off inside her sleeping bag. Silently, he ascended the staircase, not knowing quite *why* he was going upstairs in the dark.

'Must want my bloody head examining...'

It was lighter here. He tried the door where he knew Nick and Trevor were sleeping, but it would not budge. The one next door was slightly ajar, and he peered inside. Mike was lying on his back, fast asleep with a satisfied smirk on his face. His upper half was bare. Johnny's head rested against his shoulder and one long arm stretched across his chest. Jack felt reluctant to wake them. They were big men, and the blond had given every impression last night of having a temper. As such he figured that he might not take kindly to being spied upon.

Creeping back out of the room, Jack crossed to the landing window. Now that he was wider awake, he realised what had happened—the snow had drifted in front of the bay window downstairs, covering it completely and blocking out the light. He descended the stairs. It was chilly in the main room, and no wonder—the fire was almost out. Last night, he had found a plentiful supply of coal down in the cellar, filled two buckets and carried them upstairs. Now they were empty.

'Here we go again,' he grumbled to himself, grabbing the buckets. 'As if my back ain't bad enough!'

Trying not to wake the others, he tiptoed out of the room. Behind him, something creaked and he froze in his tracks, certain that someone was following him. He glanced about him, but it was too dark to see properly. Passing through the other room, he entered the scullery where there was more light. The cellar door was already open—he was sure that he had closed it last night.

Using his cigarette lighter to help him see where he was going, Jack reached the bottom of the steep, slippery stone steps when he realised that he had forgotten where the coal actually was. There was so much rubbish, so many little compartments and passages. The place also stank of cats and slime. He decided that it might be best to go back upstairs and throw some of the burnable rubbish in the scullery onto the fire instead, and had mounted the first step when he was blinded by the glare of a flashlight. He shielded his eyes, then relaxed.

'It's you! God almighty, you gave me the fright of my life!'

3: The Bungalow

Johnny awoke with a start. Either he had been dreaming, or he really *had* heard muffled footsteps on the landing—then inside the room itself.

Raising his head, he listened attentively. Beside him, Mike was dead to the world. It could not have been Mike, going to the bathroom. He would have known. Whenever Mike got up during the night he always woke him up when he returned to bed, clumsy as the proverbial camel and bouncing all over the place. All the same, he gave him a gentle nudge.

'Mike—Mike, wake up!'

His lover snorted. 'Go back to sleep, Johnny. It's too early. If you can't wait, have a wank!'

Johnny lay still. He did not feel like getting up, either, because he was so warm and comfortable—even in arguably the most dreadful bed and the most disgusting room he had ever slept in. The fire was almost out, and he knew that beyond this bed, Arctic conditions would prevail. He thought about the intrusion into their room. Perhaps it had been one of the others, straying. The door was open—just a fraction—and he distinctly remembered closing it. He had wanted to draw the bolt, or at least lean their rucksacks against the door, but Mike had said no to this. Mike hated being closed in. Then Johnny came to the conclusion that if anyone *had* wandered into the room during the night—well, maybe they might have learned a thing or two!

He snuggled up against Mike's warm, beefy body, and

tried to relax. Mike was the best thing that had ever happened to him. He was strong and protective, overtly masculine, kind, fun to be with, and the most unselfish person he had ever known. In all the time they had been together, they had hardly ever quarreled—just the odd lover's tiff, nothing more. And making up had been such fun! Fame and fortune were his, but Johnny had always found it hard coping with his new-found wealth. His first novel had caused a sensation—to cope with the success and adulation he had begun snorting coke. Mike had come along at the right moment and weaned him off the shit—Mike Brent, the loud-mouthed, brawling, boozy rugger scrum-half.

They had met in a Dublin bar, ten years ago. Johnny had just dropped out of Oxford, having suffered a nervous breakdown following the death of his mother. After his first book, success had followed success—five best-selling novels, a biography and a screenplay. And Mike had been there beside him, every step of the way. Gargantuan, steely-blue-eyed and roguishly good-looking. He too had been successful back then, a hero of the sporting world.

Within a week, they had become lovers. One night, Johnny had taken Mike back to his pad in the most exclusive suburb of the city—he had stayed there for three years, until they had decided to pool their resources, leave Ireland for good, and buy a cottage in the Yorkshire Dales. By this time, Mike's team had worked out that he licked the other side of the stamp—that 'Ten-Inch Brent' had not been thinking about clitorises and soapy tit-wanks, that afternoon they had persuaded him to get hard for charity—that he had most likely developed an erection because he had been fantasising what he might like to do to some of *them*! Matters had been exacerbated when, one afternoon in the locker-room after a match, Mike had cracked a dirty joke with one of the players, and given his cock a playful tug. Accused of sexual assault, he had been booted out of the team. The incident had made the papers, and what had made the whole affair even more hypocritical was that, six months later, the player had left his wife for another man.

Mike and Johnny had been 'out' now for eight of their ten years together, and neither had regrets or cared what the papers or anyone else in the outside world thought.

Johnny nudged him again, and his eyes flickered open. Raising his wrist, Mike checked his watch.

'Johnny-Boy, it's gone eleven. I promised the driver I'd be up at nine. You dildo—why didn't you wake me? Come on, get your arse up!'

He leapt out of the bed, rushed to the window to look outside, then pulled on his underpants. Johnny shivered—Mike had taken the blanket with him. Opening the door, he checked there was no one on the landing, and hurried to the bathroom. Five minutes later he returned, and Johnny was still in bed.

'Fuck it,' Mike growled, getting back in.

Johnny explained about the footsteps, which his lover dismissed as part of his over-furtive imagination. After all, this was an old house, and in old houses things usually *did* go bump in the night.

'It was maybe the wind blowing the shutters,' he said.

Johnny was about to explain that there *were* no shutters, but Mike's big paw had shot under the blanket and wrapped his fingers tightly about his cock.

'I'll help him dig the bus out,' he grinned. 'But I'm not going out into the cold until I've had something hot inside me. Might even have some coffee as well!'

Tom Fellows was pottering around with the fire. His spouse was still asleep, curled up on the sofa. The fire was almost out, and the ex-colonel's hands were blue from the cold. He was still feeling apprehensive about the big Irishman.

'The driver's gone,' he told Mike. 'Reckon he couldn't wait any longer.'

Mike asked him if he was sure. He tone was friendlier than Tom had anticipated, and he relaxed a little.

'Positive,' he replied. 'He went off hours ago. I thought he would have been back by now. Looks to me like he's done a bunk.'

Dave Rose walked into the room, carrying a tray on which was a selection of mugs, most of them cracked and without handles.

'I found these in the kitchen,' he said. 'I had to give them a good scrub, but at least we won't have to have our coffee in sittings. Weren't you supposed to be helping the driver? I asked him to come up and give me a shout, but according to Tom, he just left.'

'I overlaid too,' Mike replied. 'And why is it so dark down here?'

Tom wiped his hands on his handkerchief. It was no good. The fire would have to be made again from scratch.

'The snow,' he gruffed. 'Nick says it's never stopped all night. It's drifted up against the windows and doors, five or six feet deep in parts. We can't get out.'

Nick. So that was the name of the pretty-boy upstart with the posh accent—the one who had been making eyes at Johnny and humping all night in the next room with the other one! Dave pushed a mug into Mike's hand.

'It's black,' he drawled. 'Looks like the milkman didn't up this morning.'

Mike grinned. 'No sugar either—the shop was shut!'

He looked up. Johnny had entered the room. His hair was ruffled and one hand was pushed under his sweater, scratching himself.

'I swear to God I've got fleas out of that bed,' he moaned.

The nurse walked in after him—she had been upstairs to the bathroom. She looked at Mike, then at Dave.

'So, you overslept? Big deal. After all that trudging last night I could have slept for a week. And I've just looked out of the upstairs window. It's still snowing, but nowhere near as bad as last night.'

Trevor was next to enter the room. He was carrying something on a plate, and winked at Nick. Like Johnny, they both looked like they had spent the night on the tiles.

'I heard someone saying the driver had gone,' he said. 'And I just looked out of the window, too. There aren't any footsteps leading away from the house.'

'Maybe he left the back way,' Nick suggested. 'He says he knows...'

'This place like the back of his hand,' Tom finished. He tossed the piece of wood he had been using as a poker into the grate, giving up the whole thing as a bad job. 'If he *has* left, though, how did he get out? You said yourself that none of the doors would open.'

Nick did not know what to say, and Trevor chimed in, 'I never said anything when we came here but—well, didn't you think the driver was acting a little odd? I mean, if he knows the area *that* well, why didn't he drive us on to another lane and take us back into Exeter? Now it looks like we're stranded. We could be stuck here for days!'

'Stranded...' Dave pushed his long fingers through his thick, curly hair. In the half-light, his face appeared sallow. 'I think you may be right, Trevor. It's almost as if the driver brought us here on purpose. I wonder why?'

Nick laughed at this, but Trevor believed Dave could have been right. Janet was about to rebuke him for being melodramatic, but a cursory glance at Mike, rubbing his injured leg, offered her an excuse not to.

'I promised to take a look at that,' she said.

Janet grabbed her bag, a large black leather one of the type used by most medical practitioners. Mike rolled up the leg of his denims while she grabbed whatever she needed, and knelt at his feet.

'Just like Mary Magdalene,' Nick whispered in Trevor's ear, taking his hand and leading him into the kitchen where they could kiss without the others seeing.

58

Mike started when he saw Janet pick up the scalpel. 'Christ—what are you going to with that!'

Using the razor-sharp blade, she scraped away the hairs surrounding the wound, and applied the tweezers—a sharp, sudden twinge, and it was all over. She held up a shard of glass. Then she applied a dab of antiseptic ointment, and a sticking plaster.

'All done and dusted, as my mother used to say! What did you think I was going to do—circumcise you? I only do that to people I don't like!'

Mike chuckled, and thanked her. Johnny dipped into his rucksack, and spread an Ordnance Survey map across the top of the dusty dining-table. The others gathered about him as his long, perfectly manicured fingers traced the line of the Exeter to Torrington road.

'In my estimation, we're around forty miles from Exeter,' he explained, indicating the spot. 'This is where the driver turned off on to the slip-road, or at least I think it is. A house as big and as old as this ought to be marked on the map. Mike?'

Mike shrugged his shoulders. 'No good asking me, Johnny-Boy. I don't know one end of a map from the other.'

Got it!' Johnny stabbed the map with the tip of his finger. 'If I'm right, this place is either Tiddicombe Manor or Selcott House. See that big letter T, about a mile from here? That's the telephone box the driver told us about.'

Mike whistled through his teeth. 'It'll take me a bloody week to get there and back in this lot. What if the driver's found it and he's already on his way back?'

'And what if you end up getting frost-bite in that knee of yours?' Janet put in, half-seriously.

She had taken to the gay couple, and thought it about time that someone else did something for a change. Since arriving here *she* had done nothing but prepare drinks and feed them all as best she could. The driver had fetched coal up from the cellar for the fire and curmudgeonly Tom had done his utmost to keep it going. Trevor and Nick seemed like they were joined at the hip and were obviously expending their energy on other things. Kate had done little more than sleep.

'You're right,' Dave said. 'Why don't I try and find the phone box? To be honest, I could do with a little fresh air after being cooped up all night in this dusty old dump!'

'Me too,' Nick added. 'If someone could lend me a pullover or something?'

Ten minutes later, they found a window which would open—it was on the upstairs landing. Johnny forced it open and gazed at the sea of snow down below.

'A ten-foot drop and a soft landing,' he told Nick, who was wearing one of Trevor's sweaters. 'You'll be okay getting out—getting back in will be the problem. I'll have a look around, see if I can find a ladder or something.'

He and Mike helped them through the window. Nick landed on his feet, Dave on his backside, laughing and unhurt. The snow had started again with a vengeance and was now mixed in with sleet. The drifts, as the two men stumbled towards the iron gates, were thigh-deep in parts. Nick slipped down this time, and cursed loudly. He glanced

60

up at the sky, heavily overcast, with much more snow to come. It was Easter Sunday and they were stuck in a white, bleak and uncompromising Arctic wilderness.

Janet was right. There were no footprints, so the driver could not have come this way—unless of course they had been covered over. Nick got to his feet, and brushed the snow off his denims and pullover. At the top of the drive they turned left, as per Johnny's map, and were pleased that the wind was behind them and not blowing into their faces. Twenty minutes later they found the telephone box, hemmed in on all sides by several feet of snow.

'How the hell do we get inside the bloody thing?' Nick exclaimed.

Dave remembered what Mike had done to get into the house. With Nick holding him up, he managed to remove his shoe, and banged it against the glass, to no avail.

'Here, let me have a go,' Nick said.

With one almighty whack, he smashed the glass and without further ado Dave grabbed the receiver off him and dialed the emergency number. It took the operator some time to answer. Dave garbled their predicament, and the woman put him through to the police. Again, there was a lengthy delay, which served only to make him less patient. By the time someone answered, he was in no mood for beating about the bush. The policeman asked him if he had been drinking.

'No, I bloody well haven't been drinking,' he snarled back. 'I'm telling you, there's eight of us stranded in this bloody awful place, and we're snowed in. The driver had to ditch the minibus, and now he's buggered off and left us. Now get your finger out and come and get us out of here!'

He banged down the receiver—realising after he had done so that he had not told the policeman where they were. He was about to grab hold of it once more when Nick pointed ahead of them.

'Over there, Dave. Am I seeing things, or is that a house?'

It was not a house, but a bungalow, set back from the road. Dave figured this must have been the building that Trevor had seen last night. With little effort he vaulted the six-foot-high wooden gate, and by the time Nick had scrambled over the top, had already skirted the building.

'Looks like there's no one at home,' he growled. 'Shit, when will this fucking nightmare end?'

They checked the place again, this time together. The garage doors were unlocked, and they managed to drag them open sufficiently to observe that there was no vehicle inside. All the windows were shuttered, and there was no sign of any burglar alarm. To be sure, Nick rang the front bell several times, and there was no reply.

'So,' Nick sighed. 'What do we do now?'

Dave had had enough. He said, 'We do what Mike did with the house, and what you've just done with the phone box. Even if there is a burglar alarm, who the hell's going to be able to get here in this lot—unless they get the SAS to send out a helicopter? We break in, and we see if there's a phone. Nothing could be simpler!'

He could not believe he had said this! A senior partner with a firm of top-notch solicitors—and here he was, proposing breaking and entering!

This time, it was Nick who removed his shoe to smash one of the glass panels in the front door—with such crack that Dave was sure it would have been heard in the next village, wherever this was. They waited a moment before unlatching the door, just in case there was an alarm. Dave grabbed Nick by the arm.

'I hate to ask you this—but have you ever been in trouble with the police?'

He shook his head. 'No, why would you ask that?'

Dave breathed a sigh of relief. 'Because neither of us is wearing gloves, and we're going to leaving fingerprints and our DNA all over the place!'

The entered the hallway. On the floor was a pile of letters and circulars—obviously the occupants had not been home for some time. The hallway led into a spacious living-room, well-furnished but dingy on account of the snow-drifts blocking the light from the windows on either side. There were three more doors besides the one they had just entered—two led to bedrooms, one of them en-suite, the other to the kitchen. Beyond was a second bathroom.

'I don't like this,' Dave said. 'I think we just should call the cops and get out of here.'

'And I think you're worrying over nothing,' the other replied. 'You said it yourself. Not even a tank would be able to get up the hill to this place, and I don't know about you—I'm bloody starving.'

Dave grimaced. This was only getting worse. They had broken in—now his companion wanted to steal their food! He had to confess, though, that he too was hungry. And the power *was* still connected.

'Okay,' he said. 'But I think it's only fair that we should take something back for the others. God, listen to me. I'm supposed to helping to uphold the law, not breaking it!'

The cupboards were well-stocked with tins, packets and jars, though there was not much to be found in the fridge other than a few cans of beer. Dave filled two large plastic carriers while Nick raided the deep-freezer, though he was certain that it was so cold in the house where they were all hemmed in, nothing would ever defrost there. In another cupboard, he found four bottles of wine, more beer, and a bottle of whisky. Under the sink there was a large box of candles. He was hoping that there might be a torch somewhere, but was unable to find one.

'This is almost as good as going to the supermarket,' Nick grinned, grabbing a bottle and two glasses.

Dave had switched on the cooker, and was emptying something from a can he had opened into a pan.

'We might as well have a feed while we're here,' he said.

They ate well, and polished off a bottle of red wine between them. Then, while Nick was washing up and putting everything back where they had found it, Dave went into the lounge to call the police, hoping that this time he would not get the officer he had given a piece of his mind.

The telephone was not working!

'Bugger,' Nick exclaimed. 'Are you sure?'

He checked the phone, and the extension in each of the bedrooms. All the lines were dead. They searched everywhere for mobiles, not that they expected to find any.

'So,' Dave sighed. 'What do we do now?'

Nick smiled. 'Well, I *did* find a couple of things in the bathroom cabinet. I left them on the bed, through there. We've nicked their food and used their electricity. Might as well...'

Dave walked into the bedroom. On top of the duvet was a pack of condoms and a tube of KY. He turned around—Nick was standing behind him.

'Don't tell me you don't want to,' he smirked. 'I've seen that look in your eye. Mind you, I wouldn't say no to a quick shower, first. I took the liberty of switching on the immersion heater...'

Dave chuckled at this. 'You really have thought all of this through, haven't you?'

The other man shrugged his shoulders and tried to sound indifferent. 'Not particularly. Call it spontaneous reaction. Sex was the last thing on my mind when we were breaking into the phone box, and I never in a million years expected to find this place—let alone that we'd be doing a smash-and-grab! Or don't you fancy me?'

'How do you know I'm not straight?' Dave asked him. 'We don't know each other from Adam. I could be anyone for all you know—a violent ex-criminal with an aversion towards homosexuals.'

'And I could be Father Christmas,' Nick retorted. 'I think you *do* fancy me, otherwise you wouldn't look like you've got a baseball bat shoved down your trousers.'

Dave actually coloured. But Nick was right—he *did* fancy him, and he *did* want to have sex with him. Until now, the only man he had ever been intimate with had been Mick. Personality-wise, this man may not have been in the same league as his window-cleaner lover, but physically he was a walking dream. He followed Nick into the bathroom, where everything was done out in shocking pink and cream, not a decor he would have chosen for himself. The tub was of the finest porcelain, the fittings on this, the washbasin and the shower were gold-plated. An ornate gilt mirror took up half of one wall. These people, whoever they were, had great taste—yet despite the money they had spent on their home, they had not thought about installing a security system! Dave thought about this, and concluded that no burglar worth his salt would have wanted to rob a place like this, stuck in the middle of nowhere, even in summer!

Nick pulled off his sweater—Trevor's sweater—and tossed it into the bathtub, then removed his shirt. Dave swallowed hard. *What* a spectacularly hairy chest! Nick smiled, and toyed with his belt, then his zip, sashaying this back and forth several times before finally kicking off his shoes and stepping out of his trousers. The boxers he had on underneath were old-fashioned, but well-tented: white, they contrasted well with his long, lightly-tanned hirsute thighs and legs.

'He's going to want to fuck me,' Dave was thinking to himself. 'And he's probably going to make it hurt. But who cares? The guy's a stunner! Those eyes! That lopsided smile! And that dimple! I always was a sucker for a guy with a dimple!'

Nick peeled off his socks, then leaned inside the shower cubicle and switched on the taps.

'Your turn,' he told Dave. 'Don't go shy on me now!'

Dave took off his pullover. The white athletic vest he had on underneath highlighted a fine physique, not what Nick would have expected of a solicitor, sitting in some stuffy office all day, or hanging around musty court-houses. This guy looked like he worked out! And were solicitors supposed to have barbed-wire tattoos encircling their bulging biceps?

Knowing how much he was turning the other man on, Dave took his time undressing—the sex would be all the better for this. He drew the vest over his head, and flexed his pecs. These were well defined, with just a sprinkling of dusky bristles, nipples which were large and fleshy, like a woman's—one of them pierced by a tiny gold bar, yet another surprise!

'I'm going to have one hell of a job holding onto my load with this guy,' he was thinking to himself. 'And I haven't even seen his cock, yet, though I hope he hasn't had that pierced as well…'

Dave stepped out of his shoes and lost his denims—everything was tossed into the bathtub. He was wearing low-cut cream-coloured briefs—Nick thought they blended well with the decor!—and the goods within them were putting up on hell of a fight to stop them from bursting at the seams.

And Nick was also thinking, 'He's going to want to fuck me, and when he does he's going to make sure it's an experience I'll never forget!'

Removing his boxers he stepped under the near-scalding water and a moment later Dave lost the briefs and joined him—thankfully he was sporting no metalwork down below. Clinging together like limpets, ignoring their rock-hard cocks for now, they kissed, their tongues intertwining like copulating snakes. Then Dave's hand travelled south, and Nick winced as he gently squeezed his scrotum. Nick reached behind them, grabbed a bottle of shower gel and snapped the cap open. Holding it upside down under the hollow of Dave's throat, he squeezed out the contents and it trickled between their pecs and zigzagged towards their pubes. Moving apart, they massaged the gel into each other's chests—Nick's ending up by far the most lathered on account of the vast amount of hair. Kneeling down, and with the water thrashing against his back, he worked the gel into Dave's pubes, then wrapped his fingers around the thick shaft of his cock, working back the foreskin to expose the smiling head.

'Better be careful,' Dave breathed, 'If you know what I mean…'

Nick chuckled at this. Mark had been trigger-happy the first few times they had had sex, and it had *so* made working up to the second load that much more exciting!

Even so, he did not want this man exploding while they were in the shower. Kneading Dave's balls with one hand, Nick worked the other hand under his thighs and inserted the tip of his forefinger into his anus. Dave squirmed his approval, so he inserted the tip of another. Dave's cock was so rigid, it stood almost vertical against his six-pack. For a few minutes, Nick's fingers gently rotated around his anal channel, bringing a new sensation each time they brushed past his prostate.

'Feels good, huh?' he posed.

There was no need for Dave to respond to this, and he was thinking to himself, 'If he's as considerate with his cock, I can't wait for him to shove it inside me…'

Then all too soon Nick retrieved his fingers, rose to his feets, soaped his his cock and scrubbed under his pits, then rinsed off before stepping out of the cubicle.

Studying their reflections in the mirror, they toweled themselves dry, bodies steaming, cocks swaying like logs caught up in an eddy and occasionally colliding. Dave grabbed a bottle of cologne from the cabinet on the wall and was about to douse himself, but Nick forestalled him.

'You don't need that stuff,' he said. 'Don't know about you, but *I* like a man to smell and taste like a man…

They went into the bedroom, and lay side by side, on top of the duvet, gazing into each other's eyes. For Dave it felt strange doing this at ground level when the curtains were open. But who would see them—and would he care if anybody did? Last night, when he had crept upstairs to the toilet, the Irishmen's door had been slightly ajar, and he had copped an eyeful. Not only this, he was sure that the big one with the shoulder-length blond hair—Mike—had seen him watching them, and thrown him a look as if to say, 'Why don't you come in and join us?' He imagined Mike now and his boyfriend now—standing outside the window, slowly stroking each other's cocks—and this added to his excitement.

'You have the most amazing eyes,' he said.

'So do you,' the other returned, the Elvis smile sending shivers down his spine.

They kissed—not as passionately as they had in the shower, just a brushing of lips—before Nick skidded down the bed and kissed him—*very* passionately—under the balls, sucking and slurping, bouncing Dave's heavy-ladened orbs off the tip of his tongue before licking the thick pipe on the underside of his rigid, uncut cock. Dave leaked a tiny drop of precum.

'That proves that you *do* fancy me,' Nick chuckled.

'To be honest,' Dave said, 'I didn't know what to make of you at first. I even thought you might be a bit stuck up...

The words died in his throat as Nick ploughed down on him, not stopping until the trimmed bush, fragrant from the shower gel, prickled his lips. For several minutes, Dave was transported to paradise, until Nick slowly regurgitated his throbbing log.

'Stuck up?' grinned. 'I don't know about that, though I do think it's about time *you* got stuck up *me*...'

Rolling onto his front, he spread his thighs wide. Dave marveled at the smooth, broad back, a direct contrast to the astonishingly hirsute thighs and buns. Leaning across him, he nuzzled the back of his neck, and Nick shuddered as he worked his way downwards, licking the ridge of his spine, tugging the short hairs above his tailbone Coaxing him on to his knees, and he swung underneath him so that Nick's nuts rested upon his chin. Slowly, he licked the base of his shaft, before working upwards to lap the tangle of high-charged nerves under the shiny crown. Nick prepared himself to be swallowed whole—edging so badly that he half-expected to offload any second. Dave sensed this, and changed direction, inching back down the bed so that all he saw when he looked up was what he imagined might well be the hairiest pucker valley on the planet. Just two weeks into their affair, Mick had rimmed him up against the bedroom wall—for the first time, and to such an extent that he had blown his load down the anaglypta—and though this was not everyone's 'cup of tea', so to speak, Dave had *so* enjoyed returning the compliment, despite the fact that the only time he had performed oral on Bren had resulted in him being violently ill. Snaking out his tongue, he ran the point around Nick's tightly-clenched hole, which did not remain so for very long.

Nick had started to groan. 'Dave—if you don't fuck me soon, I think I'm going to go insane...'

Dave got up and knelt behind him. Squeezing out a large blob of lube, he applied it to Nick's rosebud—the guy was *so* hairy down there, it meant plastering the thick black tendrils to the rounded mounds on either side to find it! Dave rolled on the rubber and pushed his cock-head against

71

the squelchy hole, and with a hard thrust sailed halfway home.

'Fuck,' Nick exclaimed. 'I felt *that* going in...'

Dave paused, concerned. 'Am I hurting you?'

'God, no,' Nick replied. 'You *almost* made me come!'

Dave took his time. Again, with Mick he had rarely been in the driving-seat, and on the first occasion that Mick had ridden him like a champion jockey and he had offloaded after just a few thrusts, Mick had understood. Dave did not want this happening here, aware that he might not get a second chance to make amends. Withdrawing almost completely, he took a deep breath, and slid the head of his cock past the now slackened sphincter—as he did this, Nick backed on to him and he was all the way in.

'That feels so beautiful,' he moaned. 'A perfect fit...'

Sliding back and forth, his nuts waltzing high in their sack, Dave ran the flats of his hands up and down Nick's back, then under his pits, and cupped the hairy mounds of his pecs with their sharp-pointed nipples before moving downwards and fondling a cock which was so rigid, he was half afraid it might snap off at the roots. For what seemed an eternity he kept up this gentle rocking back and forth, his fingers tightening their grip on Nick's cock. Then when he sensed that Nick was almost there, he increased his speed, still wanking him like he was wearing a mink glove, until Nick grunted and sprayed a copious load across the duvet. Withdrawing slowly, Dave rolled him onto his back, whipped off the rubber, and kneeling at the side of him offloaded across his furry middle.

Lying next to each other on the bed, panting only slightly, they said nothing for several minutes. Indeed, such was the comfort here after the chilly, dusty old house that they started to nod off. Then Dave awoke with a start and glanced at his watch, and at the man beside him, his torso still streaked with jism. Two hours had elapsed since they had broken into this place, and he was sure the others would be wondering where they were.

'Seems like the driver's done a bunk,' Dave said. 'They'll be thinking we've scarpered, too.'

He tried to get up, but Nick caught him by the wrist.

'Don't you want to go again, before we set off back? Me in the saddle this time, if you like?'

Dave glanced down—Nick was hard again, and his own cock was starting to stiffen, too.

'Well, seeing as you're twisting my arm. Literally...'

Raising himself up on one elbow, he reached across and wrapped his fingers around Nick's still sticky cock.

4: The Musty Room

Johnny and Mike found a ladder in the cellar. They went down there with Johnny's flashlight *and* a candle—leaving the latter burning on the bottom step so that they would find their way back among the maze of passages. They emerged filthy, covered in cobwebs and grime, and with Johnny's pullover ripped from where he had caught it on a nail. They dragged the ladder up the steep stone steps, through the scullery, and up the two flights of stairs to the first level of the house—and Johnny wrenched his shoulder while they were hauling it out of the landing window.

Downstairs, they stripped to the waist at the kitchen sink and cleaned themselves up as best they could, washing themselves with ice-cold water and using Johnny's discarded T-shirt to dry each other—while Trevor watched through a crack in the door, his heart pounding.

'They're both so incredibly sexy,' he thought to himself, feasting his gaze on the mouthwateringly hairy chest. 'To think—last night they were doing exactly what Nick and I were doing. What I wouldn't give for a foursome with those two. I bet they're both hung like horses!'

Trevor was wondering what was keeping Nick and Dave—they had been gone hours, and he had terrible visions of what might have happened to them in this dreadful weather. Last night with Nick, the sex had been out of this world, and Trevor felt ashamed of himself for not giving Paul barely a moment's thought until now. Yet what else could he do? Everybody's mobiles appeared to be

74

on the blink, so there was no way of getting in touch. Then he had an idea. As soon as the other two returned, he would go out and follow their footprints—he would find the telephone box, call Paul, and tell him just how much he loved him and he was missing him!

Mike and Johnny put their tops back on, and Trevor moved away from the door so that they would not think he had been perving on them. Instead of returning to the communal room, they went upstairs—Mike into their room, Johnny into the bathroom where he froze in his tracks.

Tom Fellows was sitting on the toilet, with his brown corduroy trousers around his ankles. His face was blue and his eyes wide open and staring ahead of him—and the fingers of his right hand were wrapped around his cock. Johnny rushed into the bedroom.

'Mike, something terrible's happened,' he yelled. 'It's the colonel. I think he's dead!'

Mike followed him into the bathroom. Trevor and the nurse had heard Johnny raise his voice, and arrived on the scene to see what the commotion was about. Janet strode into the bathroom. She checked Tom's pulse, closed his eyes, and delivered her verdict.

'Looks like a coronary to me.'

Mike could not help sniggering at this and whispered to Johnny, loud enough for the others to hear, 'And instead of coming, he went!'

And Trevor, his eyes riveted on Tom's bell-end, suffused a smile and asked, trying not to crack up, 'What are we going to tell his wife?'

Janet shrugged her shoulders. 'She's downstairs on the sofa, fast asleep. I'll wait until she wakes up. Maybe we should send for an ambulance? Daft suggestion, of course...'

Kate Fellows was still asleep when Nick and Dave returned to the house, their cheeks suffused with colour. They had stopped off at the telephone box on the way back, and this time Nick had spoken to the police. He had given the officer details of their location, so far as Johnny had worked out from the map. Johnny and Mike helped them back up through the landing window.

'You smell nice,' Johnny could not help telling Dave, as Mike relieved them of their plastic carriers full of goodies. 'Are you sure you didn't call in at a beauty salon on your way back, as well as the supermarket?'

They explained about the bungalow, the shower—but not about the sex—and what the police had said.

'Half the county appears to have been cut off from the rest of the world,' Nick explained. 'The cop said they've sent snow-ploughs out in every direction from Exeter and Torrington. I told them there's eight people here who are feeling pretty pissed off, but they said it's going to take time to clear the roads—could even be a couple of days!'

'A couple of days,' Janet repeated. 'Shit…'

'But we're not going to go hungry,' Dave added, indicating the carrier bags. 'I don't feel particularly proud of what I've done—breaking into someone else's home and thieving from them—but I came to the conclusion we need this stuff more right now than whoever owns that place.'

'And it's no longer eight,' Trevor said. 'I think you'd better take a squint in the bathroom.'

They did, and like the others found the situation amusing. Janet had been willing to close Tom's eyes, but there was *no* way that she was touching him down there!

'Do you think we should take a picture?' Dave asked. 'I've got a camera in my bag, downstairs.'

Mike looked at him. 'That's probably the most warped thing I've ever heard...'

'I didn't mean it that way,' Dave said. 'I meant—won't the police want a picture of the crime scene, or whatever it is, before we move the body? We can't just leave him here, sitting on the pan!'

'It's not a crime scene,' Janet told him. 'He's had a heart attack. But you're right about one thing. We can't leave him here, holding *that*...'

'Yet he seems so peaceful, sitting there,' Trevor said. 'He's even got a bit of a smile on his face. God, I sound like a character from one of those *schlock* horror movies...'

'Our very own Hammer House of Horror,' Johnny echoed. 'All we want now is for Boris Karloff to come stomping up from the cellar carrying a severed head on a silver platter...'

Mike sniggered again, able to read what was going on in his lover's head—Johnny was soaking up the atmosphere, probably working out some kind of plot for his next book. And a spooky house, the central character an ex-colonel who had apparently jerked himself to death while sitting on the toilet, was certainly a better setting than

77

the caravan site scenario Johnny had originally envisaged!

'So,' Mike asked. 'Who's going to move him, and where are we going to put him?'

Dave Rose flatly refused to enter the bathroom, let alone touch the body. Not so Johnny, who in the course of his research as a crime novelist had seen dozens of corpses in a much worse state than this one—*and* sat in on innumerable autopsies, one where the body had been in the river for a week, and had broken into bits while they had been positioning it on the slab. Rigor mortis had started to set in, and not without difficulty he relieved the dead man's hand of its cargo, and with Mike lifted Tom off the toilet like he weighed nothing, pulled up and fastened his trousers, and carried him into one of the empty bedrooms where they laid him out on the floor. Janet was about to cover him with one of the Army blankets when she caught her breath.

'Mike—Johnny! Look at his neck!'

They knelt next to the body, and observed the tiny knob of metal protruding from the back of Tom's neck. Johnny touched this, and when he drew his fingers away saw that they were smeared with blood.

The snow crunched under Trevor's feet. Above him the sky was almost black. Nick had told him that it would take him less than half an hour to reach the telephone box, and he was looking forward to but also dreading calling Paul. Despite the twenty-year age-gap, Paul had until now been the most sexually exciting man he had ever known, not that he had known that many—maybe half a dozen that he had spent the night with, as many again where there had been hurried sex—in club toilets, darkened corners of car parks and the like. But last night, with Nick. That had been *real*, grinding, sweaty, satisfying man-on-man action! He and Nick had gone at it like they had invented it. Nick had made him come four times to his twice, and he was sure that if this incredibly sexy creature had not dropped off to sleep, there would have been more.

Trevor's problem was that he had always been *too* honest with people. He would tell Paul how much he loved him. Paul would say how much he was missing him—how disappointed he was that this unexpected change in the weather was keeping them apart, with perhaps no more than twenty miles separating the cottage Paul had hired for the weekend and this old house where they were snowed in, yet where he had enjoyed arguably the best rumpy-pumpy so far in his life! He would tell Paul about this—maybe he would also tell him how he had lusted after Johnny, while watching him through the crack in the scullery door—and Paul would forgive him, as he had forgiven him before.

'I'd rather share you with half the world than not have you at all,' Paul had told him, the first time he had strayed.

Plunging his hands deep into his pockets, Trevor trudged on. Despite having emptied his balls four times in as many hours, thinking about Nick—that gorgeous hirsute body, those beautiful eyes and that sensual crooked smile—had started to give him a hard-on. Last week when he had called Paul to make arrangements for their weekend together, they had talked dirty to one another while getting off. Had it not been the answering-machine earlier, he would have got Paul to call him back and done so again. After all, no one would have seen him jacking off in a phone-box in the middle of nowhere. But if the choice was between talking dirty to Paul, and saving himself for the real thing tonight with Nick—well, there *was* no choice!

Then he deliberated over whether he should tell Paul everything—about Nick, *and* about Tom Fellows...

'Hi, Paul! I'm missing you but I'm not bored. I'm stuck in this old house with a bunch of people. Last night there were nine of us, but the driver who brought us here seems to have disappeared, and earlier today we found one of the others sitting dead on the toilet with his knob in his hand. Somebody had stuck a scalpel in the back of his neck. Oh, and by the way—I've met this incredibly sexy guy, and we spent all last night fucking like rabbits!'

No, *that* did not sound right!

Trevor was thinking about what he *would* say when he came within ten yards of the telephone box, and ultimately decided that he had no idea *what* he was going to say—that wanting to call Paul had been a big mistake. Turning on his heels, he retraced his footsteps back to the house.

'Has anybody pondered where the scalpel might have come from? I mean, it's not the sort of thing you would normally pack in your luggage, is it?'

Nick glanced accusingly from one face to the other and ran his fingers through his thick, dark hair.   They were all in the room, drinking coffee laced with the purloined whisky out of cracked cups—all save Kate, who had been told about her husband, and sedated by the nurse. Mike and Janet knew the answer, but for the moment said nothing.

'He must have got it from somewhere," Dave said.

'He?' Trevor posed.

'The driver,' Dave replied. 'Who else?'

Trevor considered the possibility. Jack Gibbons had obviously gone for good—he should have been back with help hours ago.

'The driver couldn't have killed the colonel,' Johnny said. 'Tom's body was still warm when I touched it.'

'Tom was fine when we went out,' Nick elaborated.

'Unless the driver never left at all,' Mike said. 'There's always that possibility. After all, there weren't any footsteps leading from the house.'

'And here was me joking about Boris Karloff creeping upstairs from the cellar,' Johnny put in. 'I think we should search the house from top to bottom.'

Janet compressed her lips. 'There's every chance that Tom's killer *isn't* the driver, but one of us. There's also the chance that someone else is in the house, someone none of us have seen. As far as the scalpel's concerned, I can tell you exactly where it came from...'

'You,' Trevor cried. 'It was you!'

Janet laughed, nervously. 'Don't be silly. But, if we're to look at things logically, as Dave says, it could have been me—or Mike. Unless the killer's wiped the weapon clean, our fingerprints will still be on it—right, Mike?'

'Right,' he confirmed.

Mike explained how Janet had shaved the area around the wound when tending his cut knee, and Trevor apologised for jumping to such a ridiculous conclusion. Dave had reservations about Mike and his boyfriend. They were big men. It would have needed superhuman strength to plunge the blade into Tom's neck. He had not seen the body close up, but Nick had enlightened him. Tom had not simply been stabbed—the scalpel had been embedded into the bone, and so far as he knew it was still there.

And the killer had a sick sense of humour—to have wanted them all to think that the curmudgeonly colonel had wanked himself to death!

Two hours later, they ate. It was almost ten and pitch black outside, and the flickering light from the fire and the strategically placed candles played tricks on their faces. Briefly, they had talked about themselves, telling each other only what they wanted each other to know.

Kate Fellows was sleeping on the sofa—she had done nothing else since being told about her husband. Dave Rose and Janet were in the scullery, washing up.

On account of the heat from the blazing fire, Johnny had removed his sweater and was wearing just a T-shirt. He reclined in the armchair, his long legs widespread—Mike was sitting on the floor, wedged between them. Every now and then Johnny ran his fingers through his long, fair hair. Every now and then Trevor, squashed up next to Nick in the other chair, glanced across at them and was sure that

Johnny was making eyes at him. Or was this just wishful thinking?

'I don't think I've ever seen such a well-matched couple in all my life,' he thought to himself. 'They're both *so* butch. But if I had to choose it'd be Johnny because he seems so gentle and refined. He doesn't think anybody knows who he is, but I've seen his picture in the paper. It's funny how you never put faces to crime writers. You imagine them to be stuffy old men in cravats and cardigans—or old biddies with dried-up fannies and cabbage-breath. But I never knew he was gay. And what I would do, to have him just the once, to rub my hands up and down that chest! I imagine he must have an enormous cock. Must have, if it's in proportion to the rest of him...'

And Nick, seemingly reading his thoughts, squeezed his hand and whispered in his ear, 'Don't know about you, baby, but I'm feeling so horny right now, I could fuck a hole straight through that door...'

Trevor awoke suddenly, and glanced at the luminous dial on his watch. It was almost three, and he was sure he had heard something outside on the landing. A few hours ago, he and Nick had bade the others goodnight, and as he had passed Johnny, the dishy Irishman had caught his fingers in his and given them a little squeeze —a cursory gesture, but one which Trevor had found *so* electrifying.

'There's no two ways about it, he's definitely got the hots for me—and I fancy *him* rotten,' he had thought to himself, while undressing.

83

The sex with Nick had been good, though not as mind-blowing as the night before. Could this have been because he had been thinking of Johnny? Could this be why he had insisted upon penetrating Nick from behind, not his preferred position, after they had kissed and briefly sucked each other's cocks—so that he could imagine that it had been Johnny's arse that he had been sliding in and out of? Johnny was hairy—not as hairy as Nick—and Trevor surmised that if he had that much bristle above his waist, down below would be just as enticing. And *because* he had been thinking of Johnny, he had blown sooner than he would have liked—long before Nick, who he had rolled over and finished off by hand. Before they left this house, Trevor promised himself, he would give Johnny his address and ask him to send him a signed photo.

'Something nice to look at while I'm having a long, slow wank...'

Now, he glanced at the man next to him and felt more than a little ashamed. Nick was fast asleep, snoring gently, his sculptured, porcelain features illuminated by the light from the half-moon. Trevor was pleased that he had been unable to call Paul, for this house—despite its horrors—had taught him that there was a whole new sexual world to be discovered. The weekend trysts and one-night stands, before and while with Paul, had meant nothing. And he was now thinking to himself that, with Paul, he had been hanging onto a dream. He was twenty-three, in his sexual prime. Paul was in his prime too—for now. But what would things be like twenty years from now—when *he* would still

84

be in his prime, while Paul would be drawing his pension? Nick was not that much older than him, and had spoken briefly of a deep, personal sadness. Trevor wondered what this could have been. The loss of a friend or relative—or a lover, even? Thinking of Johnny while they had been having sex had turned him on beyond belief, but any day now Johnny and the others would be gone and he would never see any of them again. With Nick, he sensed that he might have some kind of future. He was thinking of this, and starting to get hard again, when he heard it again—the noise outside the door.

'Psst!'

Was this Johnny? Had that gesture downstairs signified something much more than a simple goodnight? Cautious not to awaken Nick, Trevor got out of the bed and pulled on his T-shirt, then his briefs—his cock now so rigid that the entire circumcised head protruded above the elasticated waistband. He tried to tuck it back inside, but it only popped back out again. Noiselessly, he tiptoed out of the room and on to the landing.

It was not Johnny, but Dave Rose, seemingly on his way back from the bathroom. He too was wearing just briefs and an athletic vest, and had his shoes and socks on—and his eyes at once became focused on Trevor's protruding helmet, which as if by way of welcoming the other man's interest had popped a tiny bubble.

'Very nice,' he breathed.

Reaching down, he touched the tip, and transferred the sticky substance to his lips.

'Very, *very* nice...'

Trevor moved away from the door.

'I thought...'

He was going to say that he had thought it was Johnny, and had he been able to read Dave's thoughts he would have heard him say, 'I was *hoping* it would be Nick—after all, that was my intention. But now that I've seen the goods, I'm glad it's not!'

Taking him by the hand, Dave led Trevor across the landing towards the window, where in the light from the moon they were able to better study each other.

'You're very cute,' Dave breathed.

'So are you,' the other found himself saying, taking in the lean, handsome face, the deep-set brown eyes with their long, almost feminine lashes.

Then Dave pushed one hand inside Trevor's briefs, to fondle his smooth, swollen nuts, and more of his thick, throbbing cock was exposed.

'Seems such a pity to let that very impressive hard-on go to waste,' Dave murmured.

Trevor nodded, and swallowed audibly. 'Yes—but not here where somebody might see us...'

They went into one of the empty bedrooms, and Trevor was pleased that it was not the one where they had stored Tom Fellows' body. Standing in front of the window, profile to profile and holding hands, Dave asked him he was cold.

'A bit,' he replied. 'But I've a feeling it won't be for long...'

Trevor glanced down. Dave was packing wood and he knew they would not have long, that hurried sex in a cold, musty-smelling room would be less preferable than taking one's time in an equally musty-smelling bedroom. But, as had happened on the train with Nick before they had moved on to much more exciting things, he knew that beggars could not always be choosers, and again he thought about Paul. He *would* of course see how things worked out with Nick, but time was running out—if there was any hope of them having any future together, if Nick *wanted* this, there would not be much time for talking before they all left this place. And in the meantime, why not make the best of what had started out as a bad situation, and have a little fun?

Squatting on his muscular haunches—he considered the floor too dirty to kneel on—Trevor pulled Dave's briefs halfway down to his knees, and his thick, rock-solid cock slapped back against his abs, the glistening head half-exposed from the fleshy hood and drooling already. Dave's balls, heavy and pendulous, were among the largest Trevor had seen and he presumed that, when the time came, they would produce a hefty load. Holding them up with one hand, he licked underneath them and savoured the tangy taste of sweat and machismo. Then he rolled each nut on the flat of his tongue before working his way up the turgid shaft. Slowly retracting Dave's foreskin, he watched the steam rose from the flared, purple glans. Then he bore down on the magnificent structure, taking the tip and half of the rope-veined shaft into his mouth while its owner tried not to whimper too loudly.

87

Trevor sucked him for a long time—Dave's staying power was tremendous, his meat so tasty that the younger man could have feasted on it for ever—but he eventually had to stand up because squatting was giving him cramp. They kissed again, and Trevor transferred his lips to the trimmed pits, as Dave bulged his biceps with their barbed-wire tattoos, and raised his arms above his head. Framed by the moonlight, Trevor thought he resembled a beautiful Greco-Roman statue like the one he had seen when Paul had taken him to the Louvre—save that the one in the museum had not possessed a stout, seven-inch cock and been longing to stick it inside him.

Dave fell to his knees—if he ended up covered in whatever filth was on the floor, so what? Trevor still had his briefs on, though the head of his cock was exposed above the waistband. Dave snuggled his lips against the pouch containing his gonads, and licked under the gusset. Trevor's cock, when he finally went down on it, tasted of rubber—obviously he had recently used it on Nick, the man *he* had anticipated having in this room. The fact that his cock had been inside Nick made wanting Trevor that much more of a thrill, and he swallowed the whole appendage, until his lips were buried in the thick, sooty bush.

'I'm close,' Trevor murmured. 'Better be careful. Don't want it to end just yet...'

Dave fumbled inside one of his socks and extracted two little foil packets.

Trevor grinned, 'You seem to have come very well-prepared...'

Dave gently spun him around so that he was facing the window, and pulled down his briefs.

'Now that's what I call an arse,' he murmured, fixing his gaze on the smooth, perfectly rounded globes.

Trevor's thick, powerful arms shot forwards to grip the window frame, and he squirmed as the other man daubed a blob of lube around his pucker—the area surrounding this was smooth, in direct contrast to Nick's, which had been like trekking through a miniature forest—and inserted the tip of one finger. Satisfied that Trevor was comfortable with this, Dave fed him the finger up to the third knuckle, and like a pleasure-giving probe it excavated his moist anal cavity until Dave was sure he was ready for the real thing. He rubbered up, and nudged his cock-head past the now slackened sphincter. Half-way in, he wound his arms about Trevor's waist, spread his fingers across his six-pack and began moving slowly, each thrust taking him just that little bit deeper until Trevor had taken all seven inches and Dave's trimmed pubes nestled against his tail-bone.

This was sheer heaven! Dave was thrilled that Trevor had come out into the passage, and not Nick—variety *was* the spice of life! How would he ever see Mick in the same light after today? For several minutes they did not move at all, and Dave was wondering if he would be able to shoot, eventually, while standing perfectly still. Through the darkened glass he observed their reflection as he nibbled the back of Trevor's neck, making him squirm some more. Trevor's cock, resting heavily on the sill, had begun forming a little puddle. Dave decided to wait a little while

89

before bringing him off, and moved his hands upwards, pushing them under Trevor's T-shirt to cup the smooth, solid mounds of his pecs.

They were exactly the same height, and Trevor twisted his head to one side so that they could kiss.

'It's a funny old world,' he sighed. 'Here I am, supposed to be enjoying a romantic weekend with my boyfriend, and all of a sudden all my birthdays have come at once!'

And the other was thinking to himself, 'Here was me, thinking that I was the luckiest guy in the world because once a week I got to fuck with the window-cleaner!'

Trevor had always been a bottom, and had always been more comfortable when on the receiving end of a hard, pounding tool. Last night he had practically begged Nick to service him—from behind, like this, his most preferred position—but Nick had insisted that *he* do the honours. Tonight, if they were still here in this house, which seemed more than likely—*he* would insist upon Nick being in the driving seat, and then Nick would realise what *really* good sex felt like!

Now, Dave was moving again, and Trevor's sphincter tightened its grip around his cock, making each movement that much more sensitive as he headed towards the finishing post. Trevor's cock was now so hard that it had lifted up off the window sill and swayed at a forty-five degree angle to his abs. Dave wrapped his fingers around the wrist-thick shaft, the excessive sticky precum serving as a lubricant as he began stroking him…gradually increasing speed until Trevor flung his head back and let go—his climax almost like a nuclear explosion as a good half-dozen spurts of jism hail-stoned the window-pane and ricocheted back onto his middle. Dave gritted his teeth and hung on until Trevor had finished, then withdrew his cock and lost the rubber. Trevor instinctively turned around and sank to his knees, no longer caring about the state of the floor, as Dave noiselessly and copiously offloaded across his throat and chest, drenching the front of his T-shirt.

Janet awoke early—it was barely dawn—and went into the kitchen to fill the pan for their early morning brew. Was it just her imagination, or did the tea really taste better when the water had been boiled on the fire?

She had planned on spending three nights at the hotel in Barnstaple—time enough to get to know the place which henceforth would be her nearest big town—time enough to relax before taking up her new position, nursing an old chap in one of the neighbouring villages. Now, two of those nights had been wasted in this old house, though she had in a very strange way enjoyed the experience.

An ex-boyfriend had once accused her of being a 'fag-hag', just because she liked hanging out with gay men—not by choice, but by circumstance. Her brother was gay, as were the couple who ran the nursing agency which employed her. With gay men she had always felt safe—they were not forever trying to get inside your knickers, they had impeccable taste when it came to fashion, food and culture! Last year, when she had put her house on the market in the wake of the court case—not knowing where she would be moving to, only that she wanted to get away from the accusing stares and pointing fingers—the interior decorators had been gay. They had asked permission to have their portable stereo on while working—for a week she had delighted to the sounds of Judy, Kylie and Barbra!

The old lady, her last charge. Her death had been an accident—the inquest had confirmed this—but Agnes Pinder's estranged family, who had never once visited her during her last months, had come after Janet because Agnes had left 'dear Nurse Ellis' £60,000 in her will, which they believed should have gone to them. The coroner had supported Janet. Agnes had got out of bed and fallen down the stairs while *she* had been visiting her brother, twenty miles away, and there had been a witness—the next-door neighbour, bringing a package around which had been delivered to her by mistake, who had entered the front door at the exact moment Agnes had hit her head on the bottom step. Janet had needless to say been exonerated of any part in her death, and allowed to keep the money.

Janet made the tea, but only for herself. Kate was asleep on the sofa—nothing new there—and the two gay couples had not come downstairs yet. She had no idea where Dave was, and did not really care. Of all the men in this house, she had spoken to him the least.

Dipping into her bag, Janet fished out her diary. She had bought it last year in Spain. It was of fine red leather and her closest friend—one with which she shared a closer affinity than she had any man. All her secrets were here, her innermost thoughts, the important details of a mostly mundane life. Occasionally, she had considering crossing out some contentious paragraph or other, but had always refrained. No one would ever read her diary and in any case she never let it out of her sight. Now she wrote quickly, at times her handwriting little more than a scrawl:

These two guys are so unbelievably handsome—the blond one has long fair hair and looks like a Greek god, and yesterday I caught the other one stripped off and shaving at the sink. My legs turned to jelly. In a way, it's such a waste! But, they're obviously deeply in love! They're both Irish, though the dark-haired one—Johnny—doesn't have much of an accent. As for the other one, sometimes the brogue's too strong you can't always tell what he's saying. I feel awful for writing this, but last night when I went up to the loo, their room door was open just a little bit and—well, just for a few minutes I watched them making love, and it was so beautiful that I wanted to cry...Then there's the other two—Nick and Trevor. At first I thought Nick was a little strange, almost sinister. Maybe it's because he's so posh. But I actually quite like him now. He and Trevor appear to have paired up. They're in the next room to Mike and Johnny, and when they're having sex it can be quite noisy.... Then, just a couple of hours ago I went upstairs, tried my best not to make a sound, and I saw Trevor with the other one—Dave—and they were wearing just their underpants and kissing on the landing! I don't like Dave much, though. He seems a little morose. And he's married because he has a ring on. Also he refused to go into the room when we found the colonel sitting on the loo. Maybe it's just my suspicious mind, but there was something very odd about the way he looked at me when I found the scalpel sticking out of Tom's neck. It's almost as if he knows something...

Janet closed her diary, and tucked it under her clothes in the bottom of her suitcase. She needed to use the bathroom, and went upstairs. There was no sound from the first room, but she heard giggling coming from the one next door—Mike and Johnny. A few minutes later she went back downstairs. Kate was awake, sitting upright on the sofa. She was muttering to herself.

'My poor Tom. Twenty-two years it would have been, come September...never a cross word between us. Tom was always too busy moaning at everyone else. And the funny thing is, I don't even miss the grumpy old bugger!'

Janet adjusted the cushion of rolled-up clothes, tucked this behind her, and pressed the hip-flask into her hand. It had been a stroke of luck, Nick and Dave stumbling on the bungalow—bringing back all that lovely food, and the whisky. Had it not been for them, they might all have been starving by now.

Half an hour later, Mike and Johnny walked into the room, both of them grinning from ear to ear. It had been a good night—despite there being a corpse in the next room but one. And once again when they had woken up, the door had been slightly ajar and Johnny had sworn that he had heard something on the landing.

'They call them feet,' Mike had said. 'People have them stuck on the end of their legs and they use them to get from one place to another, such as when they want to take a leak.'

'Well,' Johnny had replied. 'I still think you should have put something in front of the door. If I wanted people to watch our intimate moments, I'd hire a film crew!'

Mike had chuckled at that. 'Now that *would* be an experience, Johnny-Boy!'

A few minutes later they were joined by Nick and Trevor—the latter looking sheepish.

'Looks like his mum walked into his bedroom and caught him having a wank,' Johnny whispered.

'It snowed again during the night,' Nick announced. 'I went outside a few minutes ago—down the ladder just to check. It's starting to freeze over. Has anyone seen Dave?'

'I saw him a while back,' Janet said. 'I went upstairs...'

Trevor seemed to glare at her.

'He was coming out of the bathroom,' she finished. 'Maybe he went down the ladder too—you know, to stretch his legs. It's awfully oppressive in here.'

Janet found him, one hour later. Seemingly having got over

her loss—though the nurse put her indifference down to shock, and suspected that once the news really sank in, she would go to pieces—Kate asked Janet to escort her upstairs to look at her husband's body.

After Mike and Johnny had carried Tom into the empty bedroom and laid him out upon the dusty floor, Janet had covered him with a blanket.

'Are you sure about this, Kate?' she asked.

Janet was thinking about the scalpel. So far as Kate was aware, Tom had suffered a coronary. Nothing had been said about him having been murdered—or what he had been holding in his hand when Johnny had found him sitting on the toilet. It would be up to the police to inform her of this.

'I'm as sure as I'll ever be,' Kate replied. 'Tom never hurt me while he was alive, so I don't suppose he's going to jump up and bite me, now.'

They entered the room, and recoiled with the shock of what greeted them. Now, there were *two* bundles on the floor, both covered with blankets, one larger than the other, and the room stank like a slaughterhouse.

Janet apprehensively drew back the blanket from the larger of the two, and Kate screamed. It was Dave Rose, and his throat had been cut.

5: The Hip-Flask

Janet fetched Johnny upstairs, for no other reason than she believed he had the stronger stomach for such things.

'Believe me, it's not a pretty sight,' she told him.

Johnny whipped away the blanket. Dave was naked, and his throat had been slashed from ear to ear—so violently that his head had almost been severed. Johnny instinctively worked out also, as did Janet—the established crime-writer and the nurse—that he had been killed here, on this very spot, for though Dave's body and the blanket were drenched with blood, there was no blood anywhere else in the room. Johnny stepped back, and collided with Trevor, who had rushed upstairs after them.

'No...God, no!'

He uttered a single, piercing scream, and within seconds they were joined by Mike and Nick.

'Almighty God...'

This was Mike, who instinctively wrapped his arms about the sobbing, near-hysterical young man and half-led, half-dragged him out of the room and back downstairs.

To the six people camped out in the downstairs room, there was little difference between day and night—every minute of every hour an eternity to be endured with forbearance. They all seemed to be getting along well, apart from with Kate, who since coming here had spent most of her time here sleeping, or in a daze—hardly surprising, considering what had happened. Each had his or her own thoughts. Upstairs two of their companions lay dead—murdered, one

97

of them horribly mutilated. The near-freezing bedroom had been turned into a makeshift mortuary.

Trevor was thinking to himself, 'If only I had the guts to climb down that ladder and get away! And yet if I did, they'd say it was me—that I killed the colonel, that I cut Dave's throat. As if I would, after last night! The guy was gorgeous. I still can't believe what's happened. And if I *do* leave, I may never see Nick again...'

Janet had expressed her thoughts in her diary, '*They all seem such nice people. Only Dave seemed different—a little odd and morose. And now he's dead...*'

Johnny had helped her clean up as best they could—he really did have a cast-iron constitution—and after covering Dave with another blanket, Janet had rolled up the blood-soaked one and flung it outside, through the landing window and into the snow. Later, she had returned upstairs and wound her own expensive pale violet scarf about Dave's neck, and whispered a little prayer, the least she felt she could do to afford the man a little dignity.

Nick had fixed a shot of whisky for Trevor, and another for himself. Drinking it straight down had gone to his head, and now Nick was asleep in the armchair.

Mike, sitting in the other armchair, did not know *what* to think any more.

Johnny and Trevor were in the scullery, making tea. Despite what had happened, Trevor still had a crush on him and being close to Johnny offered him strength, though he would never recover from what he had seen in that room. Such was his fascination for the raven-haired Irishman that, had Johnny told him that *he* had slit Dave Rose's throat, and in the next breath asked him to go to bed with him, he would not have refused.

'Nick's taken it very badly,' Trevor told him. 'I suppose you know that they—you know, when they broke into that bungalow? Nick told me. And last night...'

'Last night,' Johnny repeated. 'You and Dave. Yes, I know all about that. I got up when I heard a noise. Our room door was open again. I saw you.'

Trevor carried the tray into the other room. Nick was sitting up, rubbing the sleep from his eyes.

'I ache all over,' he said. 'God, what a to-do!'

And Kate, in a rare moment of lucidity observed, 'It's always so dark down here. If only we could clear some of the snow away from the window.'

'That might have been possible yesterday,' Mike said. 'But not today. It's frozen over during the night. For all the cops care we could be holed up here for ever!'

'There's something else,' Johnny put in, sitting on the arm of the chair and wrapping his arm around Mike's neck. 'I didn't mention it yesterday because I wasn't sure. I've checked everywhere—my map's disappeared.'

'It was on the table last night,' Nick said. 'I was studying it, trying to work out where the next village is. The driver said it was twelve miles away, but we can't be *that* far from civilization? We found the bungalow—surely there must be other houses nearby—not that we saw any.'

Mike was stroking the back of Johnny's neck, and this was starting to turn him on.

He whispered in Johnny's ear, 'Bugger this malarky, Johnny-Boy. What I need right now is a bloody good fuck!'

He jumped to his feet and stretched, all but knocking Johnny off the arm of the chair.

'I don't know about anybody else, but if I spend much more time cramped up in this chair, I'm going to need a chiropractor to straighten me out, and I had enough of that when I was with the team. I'm off for a lie down...'

'I was thinking along the same lines,' Johnny said, feigning a yawn. 'Though I should imagine it's not going to be very easy relaxing up there, now...'

They had barely left the room before the others began holding an inquest.

'Do you think they're in it together?' Nick asked. 'I mean, you do know who Johnny really is?'

'Who would that be—Jack the Ripper?' Janet asked.

'His name's Johnny Rodrigues,' he elaborated. 'He's *the* Johnny Rodrigues!'

'Which means precisely nothing to me,' Janet said. 'Save that it's a funny name for an Irishman.'

'The crime writer,' Trevor added. 'I've read a couple of his books and they're quite good. A bit gruesome. Oh, my God! You don't think he's set this up so that he can write about it? And to think...'

He stopped himself from saying, 'And to think, I fancy him something rotten!'

Janet caught her breath. This put a whole new slant on things! Mike, she knew, was some sort of sportsman because he had said something yesterday, in passing, about 'the team', and again just now. He certainly had the build. But to have come here with his lover—*the crime writer*—to plan all this, the idea was way too preposterous for words.

'Why would they want to do that?' she defended. 'How were they to know the weather was going to turn—no more than the rest of us?'

Nick finished his tea. Trevor had made it too strong, but it had revived him after his nap.

'I heard Johnny telling you he'd heard someone in their room, Saturday night,' he said to the nurse. 'And what did you tell me the other night, Trev?

'The other night?' he quizzed.

'About the colonel—wandering around up there?'

'Oh, that,' he replied. 'I'd forgotten about that until now. I was coming back from the bathroom, and I bumped into the colonel on the landing. He'd just come out of one of the bedrooms and...'

'And he'd caught them at it,' Nick finished. 'That's why I put a piece of wood behind the door. Peeping Tom! Mike told me the guy was a homophobe—called him a pansy while they were on the train. It's my guess he went into their room, said something insulting—then Mike killed him with the scalpel so we'd all think it was Janet. It needed phenomenal strength, to plunge the weapon *that* far into his neck. It's as plain as the nose on your face!'

'But there's more to it than that,' Trevor said. 'Wow, this is really embarrassing...'

He looked at Kate, then at Janet, and she smiled. 'I'm a nurse, Trevor. There isn't much you could say that'd shock me. And I know what you're going to say. I was halfway up the stairs and I saw it, too.'

'Saw what?' Kate pipe, suddenly awakening from her tranquiliser-enhanced slumber. 'What was my Tom up to, Trevor?'

'I'm not sure which room it was that he came out of,' Trevor said. 'He was standing in the middle of the landing and—well, he had his cock out and he looked like he'd been bashing the bishop!'

'Bashing the bishop?' Kate repeated. 'Oh, I see what you mean. In our neck of the woods we call it spanking the monkey. I always did wonder about my Tom. He was always talking about what the homosexuals got up to in Iraq—saying that it was inevitable that they would do things with one another if they were separated from their wives and girlfriends for months on end. And yet *he* was separated from me—not that he was ever very active in that department. But those two lovely young men wouldn't have killed my Tom, would they? I should imagine they ought to have been proud that somebody wanted to watch them...'

The others stared open-mouthed at this, while Janet interjected, 'Well, my money's on the driver. I mean, we've already established that he may still be in the house.'

'And he *did* suggest coming to this house,' Nick said.

'There isn't *just* the house, though,' Kate put in. 'What about the outbuildings? The killer could be hiding there and we're making it easy for him—leaning a ladder up against the landing window so that he can get in and out!'

No one had thought of this until now...

This time, even in broad daylight, Mike was taking no chances. Throwing half a bucket of coal on to the fire, he placed the bucket behind the door next to their rucksacks.

'I don't want a mad axe-murderer barging in here and hacking me to bits while I'm on cloud nine, shooting my load,' he said, flashing his steely-blue eyes and pulling his sweater over his head and kicking off his shoes.

'And that isn't even remotely funny,' Johnny replied. 'We shouldn't really be doing this—not when there are two dead guys just along the landing and a bunch of strangers sitting downstairs. Did you see the look on their faces?'

He pulled off his own sweater and his T-shirt, removed his denims and got into the ice-cold bed.

'Well,' Mike said. 'I don't think Tom and Dave are going to want to join in—and somehow I don't think the girls may be into rimming.'

Keeping his T-shirt on, he climbed in next to Johnny, and the bed creaked. Mike kissed Johnny on the lips, then the hollow of his throat before nuzzling his dense, dark pits.

'I hate to say this, Johnny-Boy, but you're a little whiffy tonight in the underarm department, and I don't reckon I'd win any prizes for personal hygiene. Reckon we might have to skip on the preliminaries and go straight for the main course...'

Johnny sat up in the bed, reached across the top of the blanket and dipped into the pocket of his denims.

'Wet-wipes,' he smiled. 'They were on top of Janet's suitcase. I was going to ask first, but I didn't think she'd mind.'

103

He opened the packet, took out one of the tissues and wiped under his arms—fumbling under the blanket, he wriggled out of his briefs and gave his downstairs equipment a good going over too. Mike pulled off his top, and did likewise.

'These things make your cock tingle,' he said. 'Johnny-Boy, you're right. Why are we doing this?'

'Because we like it,' he replied.

'I mean, why are we doing it *here*?' he asked. 'Why don't we just climb out of that bloody window, walk to the top of the drive and just keep walking? We're sure to wind up somewhere...'

'After this, then,' Johnny said.

Rolling on top of Mike, Johnny grabbed his wrists and cruciformed his arms so that he could lick under his pits. Mike's pits and pubes were the only part of his body where he was really hairy, and he tugged at the long honey-coloured strands with his strong, perfectly white teeth, and twisted them into tiny spirals with the tip of his tongue. Mike's impressive hard-on was trying to burrow a hole through his ribcage, while Johnny's own was bent back between his thighs and digging into the dingy mattress.

Kicking the blanket aside now that they were warm, Johnny licked and kissed his lover's torso from top to bottom—slurping his tongue across each hard fleshy nipple, blowing raspberries on his six-pack, then focusing his attention on the ten-inch log which had been his alone to enjoy for the past ten years. Slowly, using just his mouth, he drew back the thick, pliant foreskin to expose the plum-sized purple head with a slit which would have easily accommodated a man's finger. Mike shuddered as Johnny slurped around the hardened ridge, then under the hypersensitive arrow-head of his glans, causing the veins in his shaft to bulge like steel ropes. He gritted his teeth, waiting for Johnny to open wide and swallow him whole, but instead he buried his lips and the tip of his nose into his musk-scented scrotum, and hummed loudly—something which he knew drove Mike wild.

'Oh, Johnny-Boy...'

Ever so gently, Johnny tugged at the folds of flesh and bounced Mike's big orbs off the flat of his tongue. Grasping the wrist-thick shaft with one hand, he bent it towards him and ploughed down on it, taking in the head and the first few inches. Sucking hard, he removed his hand and bore down again, taking all ten inches way past his tonsils.

'Oh, Johnny-Boy. I'm gonna blow...'

Johnny released him, and delivered a resounding crack across his rump which made him yelp.

'No you don't!'

Wrapping his massive arms around Johnny's back, Mike rolled him over and pinned him to the mattress. One hand shot under the makeshift pillow comprised of a rolled-up sweater, and grabbed the lube. Kissing Johnny so passionately that for a few seconds he could hardly breathe, Mike scooted down the bed and Johnny instinctively spread his muscular, hirsute thighs and raised his knees until they touched his chest.

105

'The most beautiful bum-crack in the whole wide fucking world,' he murmured, plunging his face into the black-forested trench. 'Should be designated a national monument!'

Johnny rimmed exceedingly well. Mike, less-refined and certainly less patient, preferred to pig out on this part of his lover's anatomy. Spreading Johnny's bristly cheeks wide, he spit-licked the thick black tendrils surrounding his hole every which way, and slurped around the hard ring of muscle before poking a good two inches of hot wet tongue inside. Then he alternatively sucked and dived until, when he moved away, Johnny's hole winked back at him. Even so, he applied a liberal blob of lube, and slowly inserted one, two, and then three fingers. Johnny's cock-head flared, and leaked the tiniest rivulet of juice, the most that ever happened with him before the grand finale.

Entering him was akin to a knife sinking into hot butter—just as it had been that first time, ten years ago, when such had been their eagerness that they had both exploded within seconds. Mike slid the head of his cock past his lover's sphincter, and kept going until he was all the way home. Leaning forwards, he kissed him, and for a good twenty minutes the big man moved inside him, never less than the ever-gentle giant, alternating his lips between Johnny's mouth and his pits, while Johnny's hands glided up and down his torso, every now and then digging his nails into the globes of his buttocks, urging Mike to go faster and stab a little harder, but knowing that he would not because he wanted this to last as long as possible.

And then, that final moment when they gazed into each other's eyes and Mike's big paw closed around Johnny's cock, gripping it tightly, bending it slightly towards him and chafing it but only just with the pad of his thumb. Arching his back, all but causing the bed to collapse, Johnny clenched his teeth and offloaded—the first copious spurt smacking Mike under the chin, the others spearing his sweat-lacquered chest and six-pack. Mike managed to hang on until Johnny had finished and he had let go of his cock—it slapped back against his damp, hairy belly and twitched out one final drool as Mike whipped his huge tool free of its beloved anal retreat, and thrust both arms behind his neck. As the melon biceps bulged, and Johnny's load coursed down Mike's smooth, ripped torso, so Mike's cock seemed to swell to even more alarming proportions, pointing menacingly as the head flared like an angry cobra. Without even touching himself he canoned a volley of scorching pellets which cross-crossed Johnny's torso. Then, no sooner had he finished ejaculating than he slid his cock back inside him, and enveloped Johnny in a bear-hug, mashing their abs, chests and loads together and kissing passionately once more until, finally, his cock slackened and slipped back out of its own accord.

In post-coital mood, Johnny lay with his head on Mike's shoulder. Neither had made any effort to clean up, and for what seemed like a long time, but which was effectively but a few minutes, they lay still, listening to the beating of their hearts. It was Johnny who broke the silence.

'Mike—did you mean what you said about just walking away from here, and be damned?'

'Every word,' he replied. 'I expected the caravan site to be the pits. But this place! Don't you think we should?'

'I'm not sure,' Johnny said. 'There's a maniac on the loose, but I almost feel we have some kind of responsibility towards the others. The nurse seems to have taken a shine to you, and Muscle Boy hasn't stop staring at me since we got here.'

Mike chuckled at this. 'They can fancy all they like, Johnny-Boy. You wouldn't, would you—with Trevor?'

'Not in a million years,' he replied.

'And what about the other one—Nick?'

'Not in *two* million years,' he said. 'I'm perfectly happy with the man I've got, thank you very much. But I know what you're going to say. We've all stuck together until now, and it'll make us look suspicious if we leave now.'

'Not if we all leave together,' Mike replied. 'We're all strong—well, don't know about the colonel's wife, but I'm sure we could take turns carrying her if push came to shove. It sure beats staying here like sitting ducks, wondering who's going to be next...'

They dressed, and went back downstairs. Mike flopped into the chair he had vacated a little over an hour earlier, and Johnny unashamedly sat upon his knee—well, they all knew what they had been upstairs for, so what did it matter what they might have been thinking?

Kate was saying, 'The police will have to come, now.

We'll all be questioned as potential suspects and they'll probably hold us in custody until they've finished their enquiry. Unless the killer confesses, of course...'

'Well,' Trevor said. 'If it is the driver, and if he is hiding in one of the outbuildings, he won't get back inside now that we've moved the ladder.'

'Unless he's already inside,' Janet put in.

'Yes, lurking in the shadows,' Kate said, starting to get hysterical. 'Lurking in the shadows, waiting to pounce. Watching us going through torment, ready to pick us off like flies. And if we leave, he'll follow us. He's not going to let us get away. Not now...'

Johnny whispered into Mike's ear, 'She really would make a great character for the next book. She sounds like she's stepped straight out of Edgar Lustgarden!'

Then Mike pronounced, 'While Johnny and I were upstairs, we came to a decision, but we'd like to run it past you guys. If we leave now, we should have a good three hours before it starts getting dark. We could head in the same direction, whichever direction we choose, or we could split up—say, two groups going off in different directions. Sooner or later we're bound to find civilization. We're not stuck in the middle of the Sahara. What do you think?'

'Suits me fine,' Trevor responded.

'Me too,' Nick added.

'But isn't it going to be rather different, struggling with all the luggage?' Janet asked. 'And it's very cold out there. We could end up freezing to death...

'Which would be preferable to dying at the hands of a

deranged killer,' Johnny said. 'As for our belongings, we can leave everything here, along with...'

Kate looked at him, 'It's okay, Johnny. You *can* say it—along with the bodies.'

Feeling under the makeshift cushion, she brought out the hip-flask and held it to her lips. Her fingers shook slightly, and a small quantity of the liquid dribbled down her chin and on to her cardigan.

'That's weird-coloured whisky,' Johnny began.

'Looks just like thickened pee,' Trevor added.

Janet lurched to her feet.

'Kate—don't drink it!'

She ran across the room, and tripped over her suitcase—Mike caught her and prevented her from sprawling headlong. Kate ignored the warning, and took another swig from the flask, seconds before Janet recovered her balance and swiped it out of her hand, sending it spinning across the floor.

Kate Fellows was still smiling in a confused sort of way when the first convulsion racked her body. Clutching at her throat, she tried to mutter something—her husband's name, perhaps. Then she made a loud, retching sound, as if trying to vomit back the fatal substance.

Her entire life swam before her eyes.

6: The Bathroom

Trevor Kylesworthy found the poison, thirty minutes later, by which time Kate Fellows had been wrapped in a blanket, and carried upstairs to be laid next to her husband and Dave Rose in the make-shift mortuary.

The killer had left the small, dirty, dark green bottle amongst the pots, at the side of the sink in the scullery. Using a tissue, Trevor picked it up and took it into the communal room to show the others.

Nick could barely make out the label, and passed it to Janet, who very cautiously removed the top and sniffed, then handed it to Johnny.

'As a crime writer, you may know more about this sort of this than I do—it smells like cyanide, to me.'

Johnny smelled the top of the bottom, and nodded. 'Prussic acid—and *this* was in your hip-flask?'

All eyes were now fixed on Janet's face, and the nurse found herself shaking.

'Where did it come from. *Who* left it there for us to find?'

She sensed that she was wasting her breath. They were *all* staring at her, now. She fought back the tears—she had been fond of Kate, despite her persistent twittering, and felt angry that they could suspect her of such a heinous deed.

'Don't look at me like that! It wasn't me!'

Nick was the most accusing. 'You've been feeding her from that hip-flask since we got here. I saw you with it on the train...'

111

'If I'd have wanted to poison her, I wouldn't have tried to stop her from drinking out of it,' she cried. 'For God's sake, stop being so ridiculous. I didn't even give Kate the flask, this time. I left it next to the sink last night, after I'd rinsed it out. Either she filled it herself—though God knows she wasn't that dippy to think a bottle like that contained whisky—or one of you lot gave it to her!'

Their expressions seemed to change now that the boot was on the other foot!

Trevor pronounced, bitterly, 'First the colonel, then Dave. And now the grieving widow. You bitch!'

Janet felt like grabbing hold of the silly boy and shaking some sense into him.

'I didn't kill her, you stupid sod! I didn't kill anybody!'

She slumped into the armchair, and sobbed—and as if on cue, Johnny and Mike rushed to comfort her, each perching an arm of the chair, each taking a hand.

'Ignore him,' Johnny said.

'Stupid little prick,' Mike barked. 'I've half a mind to...'

Trevor placed the bottle on the table.

'I'm sorry,' he told her. 'That was irresponsible of me. This place is getting us all het up and I should learn when to keep my mouth shut.'

'Yes, you should,' Nick put in. 'I think we're all saying and thinking things we shouldn't. Anybody else would be the same. For what it's worth, I'm with Mike—what he said earlier. I think we should leave, before he kills us all...'

'The driver,' Johnny sighed. 'Obviously he *is* still somewhere in the house, seeing as we've shifted the ladder.

112

My money's on him being down the cellar, or up in the attic. Maybe we should do a thorough search...

'Rather you than me, Johnny-Boy,' Mike said. 'What happens if he's armed? I think we should just sit it out and stick together until morning. It's too late to leave, now. We'll get no further than the end of the lane before it gets dark. Did anybody notice any street-lights when we were on our way here the other night?'

'On the main road, I think,' Nick replied. 'I'm not sure about the slip-road, though I should imagine so. There certainly weren't any on the way to the bungalow.'

'Well,' Trevor said. 'I guess the safest thing to do is to do what Mike says and make sure none of us are left on our own—and to bolt the doors to our rooms.'

'Better still that we all sleep downstairs in this room,' Mike responded. 'Seeing as it's going to be our last night here. Janet can have the sofa. I don't mind kipping down on the floor—can't get any muckier or smellier than I am already. What I'd give right now for a hot shower!'

'Which reminds me,' Nick put in. 'With all the fuss and upset, I forgot to say that we actually have hot water here.'

'Oh,' Janet asked, starting to come around a little now that they had all seemingly stopped suspecting her of being a serial killer. 'How's that, seeing as there's no power?'

'Tom found one of those old-fashioned dampers halfway up the chimney-back,' he explained. 'It was all caked up in soot, and he cleaned it. There's a back-boiler, like the ones they used to have years ago. I had a wash and shave earlier—the water's piping hot."

'Well,' Mike said. 'I think I'd rather pong for a little while longer than risk having a bath up there. You never know what might come crawling out of the plug-hole. But if anybody else wants one, Johnny and me can stand guard outside. How about you, Janet?'

She had dipped into her suitcase for her hairbrush, and was dragging it through her long, red mane. Once, in pre-Johnny days, Mike might have shown interest in such a woman—now, she reminded him of the Madwoman of Lammermoor he had seen last year while they had been in Milan, and Johnny had dragged him along to La Scala.

'Later, perhaps,' she said.

Trevor, who had just thrown coal on to the fire, raised one arm and sniffed his pit.

'I'll be the guinea-pig,' he offered. 'But I'm not going up there on my own. Nick?'

Johnny and Mike exchanged glances and Mike winked as if to say, 'Well, we can hardly say anything—seeing as not so long ago we went up there for a bit of how's your father!'

Nick had cleaned the bath, after his wash and shave. The floor was filthy, but Trevor put this to rights by spreading a blanket across it. He had also brought the obligatory condoms and lube. Johnny had loaned them his towel, and this in itself made Trevor feel horny—the fact that he would be using something which touched Johnny's body, intimately, to dry his own.

It was only three in the afternoon, but already starting

114

to get dark outside. Trevor wondered what it would be this time—snow, or rain—as he pushed the plug into the hole and switched on the taps.

When the bath was half-full and the room swirling with steam and that much warmer, they undressed, pausing to kiss after each item of clothing had been discarded and dropped into a heap in front of the door. Nick had already stepped into the tub when he realised he had forgotten the shower-gel and soap.

'I have some in my suitcase.' Trevor said. 'Won't be a tick. Try not to start without me!'

He wondered whether or not to wrap Johnny's towel around him, then decided not to. It would take him no more than ten seconds to fetch the items they needed. He stepped on to the landing and was swinging an impressive semi when he saw Mike coming up the stairs.

'Nice piece of meat you have there, Trevor,' he quipped, and even had the audacity to give his cock a little squeeze. 'Make you sure you put it to good use, son!'

Trevor grabbed the soap and gel from his bag, and went back into the bathroom. For a moment he wondered what would have happened, had that been *Johnny* out on the landing—what his reaction would have been if *he* had squeezed his cock—and thinking about this suddenly made him feel hornier than ever. Then he reminded himself that Johnny would almost certainly never have done such a thing as grab his cock, that even if he had, those two were *so* joined at the hip, nothing would have come of it. And in any case, Mike had only been larking around—he assumed.

There was a large iron bolt on the door, and for a moment Trevor thought about drawing it across. Then he remembered what his mother had drilled into to him as a child—about never locking the bathroom door in case the house caught fire. He stepped into the tub. It was a large one, but still only big enough to accommodate them kneeling, facing each other, their cock's hard and their helmets touching, the slits in them kissing, ready for action.

'Young, hung, and full of cum,' Nick mused. 'Have you never wondered what it'd be like, having a foreskin?'

Trevor shrugged his shoulders. 'Never thought about it. Have you wondered what it'd be like, *not* having one?'

Nick chuckled at this. For a few minutes they allowed the cocks to engage in a little friendly swordplay, as their leaden nuts swung from side to side. Then Trevor shaved, and they washed each other's hair and massaged shower-gel into each other's bodies—Trevor working up quite a lather on Nick's chest, pits and abs on account of all the hair. He had to stop Nick from working it into his cock, however, fearful that he might make him shoot so soon.

'One of the most magnificent cocks I've ever seen,' Nick murmured. 'Do you realise, apart from the fumble on the train—which was exceptionally nice, by the way—this will be the first time you've fucked me in broad daylight?'

Reaching down, he fondled and tenderly kneaded the young man's balls, then working underneath his scrotum located his pucker. With little difficulty, he inserted the tip of his finger. Trevor clenched hard on this, looked him in the eye, and grinned like a sheep.

'Save that this time, *you're* going to fuck me...'

Nick smiled—the lopsided Elvis expression, and ever so sexy. 'Fair enough. I've been on the receiving end of that gorgeous monster ever since we got here. And I've been thinking, once we get away from this place. We live fairly close to each other, up North. I think we should take this to the next level. It's been a while now since my boyfriend died. Mark was killed in a car crash, last year—a drunk driver. For a long time, I thought of nothing else but joining him. We were *so* in love. Then after what seemed like an eternity of one-night stands, morning I woke up and told myself it was time to move on. Time to settle down. That's what Mark would have wanted. I never asked you before, but are you—attached?'

Trevor shook his head, and felt no shame in doing so. Since coming here he had hardly ever thought about Paul, and it was almost as if he was already a distant memory. He closed his eyes—partly to envisage his lover's face and forty-three year old body, which he had never had cause to complain about so far—largely because Nick's finger was still rooted deep inside him, and he was thinking to himself that if just the tip of his *finger* felt so good, how good would it feel taking seven inches of cock? He also felt proud that Nick had wanted to confide in him something so unbelievably sad about his personal life, his eyes brimming with tears and his voice breaking while doing so. Never in his life had he met a man who seemed so *utterly* sincere!

'I'd like that,' he said. 'Actually, there *was* someone, but not any more...'

117

Climbing out of the bath and leaving the water in so the room might stay warm a little longer, they stepped on to the blanket and took turns to dry each other, using Johnny's towel. It smelled of his perfume, of his manliness, but all of a sudden, Johnny was no longer important—just another unreciprocated crush. Nick wanted them to see each other again when they returned home!

Like a blind man sees by using his fingers, Trevor closed his eyes once more and used his lips to explore every contour of the other man's face—the deep-set eyes, straight nose and sculptured cheekbones, the dimpled chin, the resolute jawline. Then, their bodies still steaming, they held each other in a tight embrace, and kissed so hungrily that they almost choked. When they finally broke away, there were tears in Nick's eyes once more—understandably, after what he had been through. He was a big man and by no means a weakling, but Trevor instinctively nurtured the need to protect and care for him. Whatever had happened in the past, or what was happening right now within this awful house where a psycho killer lurked among she shadows, Nick need never feel afraid again—for as long as there was a breath left in his body, *he* would take care of him!

Squatting on his haunches, his cock rigid against his hairy abs, Nick kissed the inside of the smooth, muscular thighs, forcing Trevor to stand feet slightly apart while he worked upwards, nuzzling his balls as the heavy, hoodless log bounced off the bridge of his nose. Taking his time, he traced his lips the full length of the rigid pipe until they reached the hypersensitive tangle of nerves under the glans, forcing Trevor to leak a little juice, which Nick lapped up like a starving man. Nick had always loved giving head, and almost always swallowed—for it was better for the guy on the receiving end for the guy delivering the blow-job *not* to stop at the crucial moment, was it not? Trevor bent his rope-veined cock downwards, wrapping the fingers of one hand around the shaft and keeping them there so that Nick could not over-gorge on him—he wanted to hang on to his man-juice until that hairy poker was deep-rooted inside him and taking him to heaven and back.

'Man,' he moaned. 'You sure know how to suck cock. Are you as good when it comes to eating pussy?'

Dragging his cock free, and not a moment too soon to prevent himself from exploding, Trevor turned around, and stuck his rump in Nick's face. This Nick had very definitely *not* expected. Though almost all of his lovers had been overtly fond of applying tongue to anus, he—as the perpetual bottom—had never had the desire to try and did not relish doing so now. He could probably count the number of times he had fucked a man on the fingers of one hand—well, maybe on the fingers of both hands, and though he had connected finger and even big toe with sphincter many times, this was something new. Yet he was committed, and knew he would have to soldier on. Apprehensively, he buried his nose between the firm, dimpled globes—so far, so good. Using just his thumbs, he spread Trevor's cakes wide and as he did Trevor backed on to him, causing his sphincter to collide with his pouted lips. Nick was pleasantly surprised. The bouquet was musky and the taste manly and little different than what he had just savoured while nuzzling Trevor's nuts. Still cautious, he risked poking out his tongue and flicked it against the hard, damp ring of muscle and the younger man flinched.

'Wow,' Nick exclaimed. 'I never knew it'd be as good as this. It just tried to bite me!'

Trevor giggled, like a giddy schoolboy. 'Nick—are you telling me this is the first time you've eaten arse?'

'The first, but not the last,' he purred. 'It tastes just like chicken, only better!'

For several minutes, Nick's tongue cruised up and down this exciting new territory, slurping from the hardened ridge behind Trevor's ballsack up to his tailbone, then back again—lingering just a little longer, each time he passed it on his travels, to poke the point of his tongue just that little bit deeper inside the hole, until it gaped wide open, purple, wet and inviting.

Snapping the cap off the lube, Nick squeezed a blob of the stuff on to the tip of his finger, and swabbed it around Trevor's crack. A moment later he was rubbered up, praying that he would not let Trevor—and himself—down by finishing before he had even started. Positioning the teat of the condom against the russet-coloured bud, he pushed gently and was surprised at how easy it was sliding all seven inches home.

'Oh—that feels *really* good...'

Once inside, he paused for a whole minute, held his breath and bit his lip, while Trevor sensed his apprehension and tried not to grip too hard. Once the urge to explode had diminished, he sashayed back and forth, clamping his hands around Trevor's rhythmically swaying hips as he backed onto him, matching his movements thrust for thrust. Trevor stooped forwards until he was almost touching his toes, enabling Nick, now that he was more in control, to venture stabbing just a little harder and deeper. He kept this up for a good ten minutes, surprising himself with his endurance, until gripped once more by the urge to let rip. For a little while he stemmed the flow by reaching around and grasping Trevor's granite-hard cock. For the younger man, this was too much—he, who until now had believed himself possessed of a herculean staying power, tottered on the brink of nirvana as Nick took over and slammed into him like a man possessed while his right hand jerked him with equal fury, each downward stroke banging against his balls. This was how fucking *should* be! A moment later they offloaded together, and not without a great deal of noise—Trevor torpedoing his jism beyond the confines of the blanket and splattering the wall, while Nick raised him onto his tiptoes and almost up off the floor as he all but blasted the teat off the condom.

It was after ten. At home, they would have been relaxed in front of the television—or maybe out drinking at their local pub in the Yorkshire Dales. Now, Mike was sitting on one side of the sofa, with Johnny sprawled across it and with his head in his lap. Both were asleep—there was little else to do here, and they had agreed to take it in turns to keep watch, and listen out for the slightest movement outside the room. Janet had removed the bottle of poison, which she assumed would have fingerprints or traces of the killer's DNA—using a handkerchief to pick it up, she had put it in a plastic bag and hidden it in the bottom of her suitcase. Then, as an afterthought she had removed it, sealed the bag with sticking plaster to make it watertight, and sneaked it upstairs where she had taped it under the lid in the lavatory cistern. Now, she took out her diary, and started to write:

Three people have been killed—murdered by a maniac. A paranoid schizophrenic. Mike thinks he may be hiding up in the attic or down in the cellar, and I tended to agree at first. The colonel was killed with my scalpel—he'd taken it from my medical bag. Something else was used to kill the solicitor because when I checked, the scalpel was still embedded in Tom's neck...The cuts were very deep and expertly done. Trevor—that's the young man, I'm not sure what he does for a living—was beside himself with grief. Those two obviously had something going—yet he seems to have got over it very quickly, too quickly for my liking. The most audacious killing was that of the colonel's wife—right in front of our eyes. The killer put poison in my hip-flask! I'd left it on the side in the kitchen, so it could have been meant for any one of us .Just now, they blamed me, but I think that was just anger. I just wish the police would come before anything else happens. Of course, the whole murky

*you-know-who episode will be raked up again.
That's a slur I'm going to have to put up with for a
long time. But this time there'll be no pointing
fingers because I know who the killer is—I saw
something!*

It was Easter Tuesday morning. Janet awoke at first light.
Despite the adverse weather conditions, outside the window
there was a dawn chorus. She was chilled to the bone—the
fire had burned low. Mike and Johnny had wanted her to
sleep on the sofa, but she had still preferred the floor and
the comfort of Johnny's sleeping-bag. *They* were far too big
to sleep cramped up in armchairs and had somehow fit onto
the sofa, sleeping top-to-tail without falling off.

Janet studied the sleeping forms. She had never seen
two men so well-matched, two men so—*beautiful*! Both
sported a quarter-inch of stubble and neither had seen soap
and water since coming here. Their clothes were dirty.
Johnny's hair looked greasy, as if had not seen a comb for a
month. Yet they *still* looked amazing, like a pair of matinee
idols who had just walked off the set of an action movie!

Yesterday, Mike had decided—for all of them—that
they would be leaving today, straight after breakfast,
whatever breakfast would be. They had agreed a time—ten
o'clock. It was now just after six. She reached into her
suitcase for her diary. At home, she kept it on the table next
to her bed, and sometimes, first thing on a morning, she
wrote down what she had dreamed about during the night.

The diary was not there.

Janet was wondering what to do when Nick walked into the room. He and Trevor, no longer making any secret of their relationship, had slept upstairs—Trevor had placed a bucket of coal behind the door, and had leaned an iron bar against the wall next to the bed—he had found this when he and Nick had gone down into the cellar to fetch the coal.

'Somebody sounds happy this morning,' he smiled, nodding towards the window and meaning the cacophony of birds outside. 'And talk about a change in the weather. Didn't you hear it raining during the night?'

On the sofa, Mike stirred, and yawned.

Nick explained, 'I was taking a leak when this bloody great chunk of plaster dropped down from the ceiling—missed my head by inches. Must have been loosened by all the steam coming from the bath...'

Mike chuckled, 'Serves you right for not pissing in the sink the same as everybody else...'

'That's awful,' Janet said. 'You could have been...'

Her voice trailed off as Nick went on, 'There's a big hole there now. You can see right through, up to the roof where the tiles are missing.'

Johnny was awake now. Sitting up, he coloured and pulled his sweater down over his middle.

'Johnny-Boy,' Mike whispered. 'A little dickie-bird tells me you've got morning wood. I know we should have slept upstairs...'

'But that's a good thing, isn't it?' Johnny asked. 'The rain, I mean. It'll have washed the snow away. We might get wet, but at least walking will be less of a trauma.'

It was Trevor who replied, half-walking, half-shuffling into the room, looking unkempt and rough, as though he had had a bad night.

'Unfortunately not, guys. It's starting to freeze over—looks like a skating-rink out there.'

'Skating-rink or not,' Mike growled, 'Johnny and me are leaving as soon as we've had something to eat—and Janet's coming with us!'

The nurse smiled at this. She could not wait to get away from this awful place. If only she could find her diary. The missing red leather tome both niggled and worried her. Janet had written things in that book which should never have been committed to paper in the first place. The inquest, and the sordid events leading up to it. Her love affairs, and those of some of her charges, along with personal details about their lives and financial circumstances. Her thoughts about Johnny and Mike were there too—she had written of how, through a crack in the door, she had watched them having sex. And most fearful of all, she had described something else she had seen—the one little detail which might prove the killer's undoing.

Hoping that this might calm her nerves, Janet decided that she would go upstairs and take a bath. Mike asked her if she needed him or Johnny to stand outside on the landing and keep watch, and she shook her head. In broad daylight, she assumed, there was nothing—or no one—to watch out for. And in any case there was a bolt on the bathroom door, so she would be safe—though as extra precaution she had a pair of scissors in her medicine bag, and rolled these inside

125

her towel. Even so, Mike escorted her up the stairs. Then he returned to the others. The coffee had run out, and Johnny had made yet more tea.

'If I don't see another fucking cup of tea as long as I live, it'll be too soon,' Mike growled.

They drank their tea, and chatted about this and that. Mike had decided for them that they would make their way to the bungalow, and stay there until the police came to rescue them.

'We should have thought about this before,' Trevor said. 'Okay, so it's breaking and entering, though I guess that technically we'd be entering a place that had already been broken into.'

'And what can the cops do?' Johnny put in. 'All they'd have to do is check what's happened here, and they'd see that we had no choice.'

'At least we'd be warm,' Nick added, 'Though there's not much food left. Dave and I nicked it all. Unless the owners have come back. Then we wouldn't have to break in at all and they'd think they'd been robbed by someone else. It would all be perfectly legit!'

One hour later, Janet had not come down. Mike went to the bottom of the stairs and shouted her name. When there was no reply, he rushed upstairs and tried the door.

'Janet—have you fallen down the plug-hole?'

There was no response. Johnny joined him, and hammered on the door with his fists, skinning his knuckles. Nick was now standing on the landing, with Trevor at his heels, like a faithful puppy.

126

'She must have bolted the door and fallen asleep,' Nick said, applying his shoulder to the door.

The door would not budge. Trevor tried, but the result was the same. Johnny's hand was bleeding.

'I'd get that seen to if I were you,' Mike told him. 'Leave the door to me...'

Johnny went into their room. He had a pack of elastoplast in his rucksack, and was in such a hurry to find them that he just tipped the entire contents of the rucksack onto the bed. He found the elastoplast, quickly tended to his swollen knuckles, and was on his way out of the room when something stopped him in his tracks. There, amongst his belongings, in the middle of the bed, was Janet's bright red leather diary! Instinctively he knew that something bad had happened to her.

He rushed out on to the landing just as Mike Kung-Fu kicked the door in. They cut through the clouds of steam. Janet Ellis was still lying in the bath, the wrong way around and facing the door. She was naked, and her eyes were still open, staring up at the hole in the ceiling. Attached to the taps and wrapped tightly around her throat was the violet scarf which Johnny had last seen covering the wounds in Dave Rose's neck, after they had laid him out.

7: The Thaw

They had checked the bathroom door. Janet had not drawn the bolt, unable to do so because it had been stuck through years of rust. On the floor were a pair of medical scissors, which she had obviously wedged under the bottom of the door to prevent anyone from getting in.

'So,' Johnny sighed. 'She decided to take the easy way out. She knew we were on to her.'

He had never touched a naked woman before, and once the water had drained out of the bath, he and Mike lifted Janet out and dried her as best they could, using the blanket which Trevor had spread on the floor, earlier. After carrying her into the other room and laying her next to the others, they went back downstairs.

Johnny showed everyone the diary he had found in his rucksack, and sitting or standing around the table they went through it, cover to cover. Several pages had been ripped out, including those containing entries she had made during the last few days.

'I was certain it was her,' Trevor confirmed. 'Somebody—I can't remember which one of us it was—said that whoever killed the colonel must have been super-strong to shove the scalpel so far into his neck. She would have known where all bones and things were, wouldn't she—her being a nurse? She would have known exactly where to shove the scalpel in.'

'I guess so,' Nick responded. 'But what about Dave? If it was her, what did she use to kill *him*?'

'I would suggest the scalpel again,' Johnny told him. 'I

saw the wound. It was—well, very expertly done. There's a box of tools in the scullery. The scalpel would have been slippery and hard to dislodge from Tom's neck—but not if the killer used a pair of pliers.'

'So, Miss Marple—that's our case solved,' Mike said. 'But there's one thing we've overlooked. What happened to our friendly driver?'

Trevor shrugged his shoulders. 'I guess we were right with our original theory. He did a runner...'

'Leaving no footsteps,' Nick finished. 'No, it's my guess she did him in too. Don't ask me why. Don't ask me why she killed any of them. It's quite obvious from reading her diary that she had some sort of mental problem. No, I think the driver's here—somewhere in this house. The question is, where has she hidden him?'

They searched every one of the upstairs rooms. They checked cupboards, closets and ante-chambers, looked under the beds and even tapped the walls for evidence of secret panels. They checked to see if any of the floorboards had been raised, and each time drew a blank. The trap-door leading to the attic was immediately above the bed where Mike and Johnny had been sleeping. Mike fetched the ladder and checked this—it was stuck and he could not budge it.

'That's it,' he said. 'I'm off out there to find that phone.'

'I'm coming with you,' Johnny told him.

Mike shook his head. 'There's no need, Johnny-Boy. No need for anybody to come with me, now. We've all stuck it out here for this long. A few more hours isn't going to make much difference. Our killer's topped herself. If you come with me I might insist that we keep on walking, and that wouldn't be fair on the others. After I've called the cops I'll head for that bungalow. If the owners have returned—well, maybe they'll take us in until help arrives without us having to invade the place like squatters.'

'They'll understand,' Trevor told him. 'Mike would only have to explain what's happened here, and they'd help us. We could offer to pay for the damaged door and the food we've been eating. There must be money in this house without having to use our own. Perhaps if we check everybody's pockets, upstairs...'

'You mean steal from the dead?' Johnny asked. 'Isn't that a little despicable, Trevor?'

'Despicable, my left tit,' Mike put in. 'Great minds think alike. They won't be needing any money where *they've* gone to...'

Mike was delighted that the thaw had begun. It meant of course that everything was cold and mushy underfoot, and the wet soon penetrated the thin soles of his shoes and made his toes numb. The roads were starting to clear. He imagined they would all have to stay in the house until the police and the forensics people arrived, and maybe it *had* been wishful thinking to suggest that the owners of the bungalow would be in a charitable mood if they had returned him to find that their home had been broken into.

He saw the telephone box, but before reaching it crossed the road and kept on walking...having observed the bungalow in the distance. He would try this first—after all, *he* could not be held responsible for what Dave and Nick had done. Through the broken pane in the front door, he saw the pile of letters and circulars. Obviously the owners were not back yet. He shouted out first, as a precaution. Opening the door, he cautiously entered the building, and checked the place out as thoroughly as any cat burglar might. The telephone in the living room was still not working, and he checked the extensions in the other rooms, to no avail. Towels had been slung on the bathroom floor, and in the ashtray on top of one of the bedside cabinets were two used condoms.

'Interesting,' he mused.

Mike checked his watch—it was almost half-past one, and he was hungry. In one of the cupboards he found a can of baked beans and sausages, and under the sink, a pan. He had to think twice about what he was doing—when Dave and Nick had come here the place had been snowed in and there had been no chance of them being caught. What if the owners returned, now that the roads were starting to clear?

'Aw, fuck it...'

He emptied the food into a pan, and placed this on the stove. Then, eating from the pan with a spoon, he walked into the room which overlooked the front drive to the property, just in case, thinking that if the owners *did* come back, he would be able to make a quick escape via the back door and maybe cross the adjacent field which would take him back to the road. He then returned to the bathroom, and had a proper wash, at the sink, before leaving.

When he reached the phone box, he observed the broken glass—the only way the other two had been able to reach the telephone on account of the snow. Now, the wire had been cut and the receiver lay upon the floor.

Cursing to himself, he made his way through the slush back to the house. It was just after two o'clock when he reached the top of the drive.

Trevor had made tea, which they had been compelled to drink without milk *or* sugar, and now they relaxed in front of the fire—actually relaxed, side by side on the sofa. Johnny had gone upstairs—for a lie down, he had said.

With tears in his eyes, Nick told his new lover about Mark—confiding even the most intimate details, and of the devastating effect his death had had on him. For weeks, apart from attending the funeral, he had not left the house and had only returned to society and a half-normal life when in danger of losing his job. Trevor offered a sympathetic ear, and opened up about Paul, a man old enough to have been his father.

'Age makes no difference at all,' Nick said. 'Well, if you were nineteen and he was ninety, it might. Mark was four years older than me. It's what's in here that counts.'

With this he touched his heart, and urged Trevor to lean against his shoulder.

'Do you really think we could make a go of things, you and I? Or were you saying that to make me feel better and get inside my pants?'

Nick giggled at this, 'I didn't have to say much at all to

get inside your pants on the train, did I? Yes, I do think we might have a future. You seem like the faithful type, and I've always been a stickler for fidelity. Mark and I were together a long time, and we never even looked at anyone else. Ours was a love that should have lasted a lifetime. Okay, so I said that age should make no difference, but I was being a little economical with the truth. My father's twenty years older than my mother, and he's often mistaken for *her* father. I still don't know that much about you, but what I do know is that a vibrant young thing like you shouldn't be tied down to an old codger!'

Nick kissed the side of Trevor's face, and glanced down. The boy was packing wood!

'I know,' he sighed. 'It happens all the time when I'm near you. Aren't you feeling horny, too?'

Nick rewarded him with the Elvis grin. 'We could go upstairs, if you like—but I have the sneaking suspicion Mike will be here any minute, maybe with the police if he's managed to get through to them. And Johnny's up there, remember? Best to save it for later, when we've found ourselves a nice comfortable hotel...'

'A proper bed,' Trevor sighed. 'I think I've forgotten what one of those feels like!'

'But I don't think this bare-headed fellow's going to be able to wait until then, is he?' Nick asked, spreading his fingers across the other man's bulging crotch.

Trevor stood up, unbuckled his denims, dropped these and his briefs to his ankles, and sat down again. His turgid, cut cock slapped back against his sweater and he made as if

133

to pull the garment over his head. Nick forestalled him.

'Just relax. Let me do all the work...'

It was to be rapid relief as Nick leaned across his lap, allowing his tongue a few cursory laps around the sticky, musky-tasting pulsating helmet before bearing down and taking a good half of the shaft into his mouth. Trevor groaned—after just five minutes of intense gorging, Nick had him on the edge. Then, regurgitating his meaty prize, he sat up and wrapped his fingers around the spit-drenched weapon. Seconds later, Trevor's copious load spurted high into the air, most of it landing back in his pubes. Nick chuckled, went down on him again, this time taking his entire cock to the back of his throat. Then, satisfied that Trevor had finished burping, using the tip of his tongue he hoovered up the jism from his bush.

'Short, but sweet,' he murmured, licking his lips.

Trevor lay back with his head on the arm of the sofa, while Nick got up and returned the tea cups to the scullery. A few minutes elapsed, and Trevor's cock showed no signs of softening—just as he had expected, with Nick bringing him off so quickly. Closing his eyes—and not really caring whether Johnny walked into the room or not—he toyed with his sticky pole and reflected on what Nick had just said, about them finding a hotel room—and on what he had said before, about them seeing more of each other when they got home. Nick was right. Paul *was* too old for him. And how would sex between him and once-a-night Paul ever be the same again, after the past few days with this equally priapic hairy and almost fiendishly handsome stud?

Then he was brought back to his senses by the sound of crashing crockery, coming from the scullery—followed by a deep, agonising moan.

Tucking his cock into his briefs, but unable to properly fasten his denims on account of his hard-on, Trevor rushed into the scullery. The cellar door was wide open, and Nick was lying face-down on the floor in front of it, among the smashed contents of the tray, his head in a pool of blood.

'Dear God, no...'

For a moment, Trevor froze. In the space of a few seconds he saw his future evaporate—the plans he and Nick had made together, all of them evaporated now. The man he had known but a few days, yet who he had instinctively sensed—call it intuition—might just turn out to be *the* great love of his life. Mike and Johnny had told everyone—the other night while they had been sitting around the fire and sharing anecdotes—of how they had met purely by chance, on what could have been a one-night stand, since which time they had not spent a single night apart in the ten years which had elapsed since then.

'Theirs is a love affair made in heaven. Mine and Nick's could have been the same...'

He started, thinking he had heard a noise behind him—Johnny perhaps, rushing down the stairs to see what the fuss was about—but when he turned around no one was there. Then he observed the box of tools in the corner, and remembered what Johnny had said about the killer—the nurse, he had assumed until now—having to use a pliers to pull the scalpel out of Tom's neck. There was a hammer—a heavy claw hammer—and he picked this up. Then he also remembered seeing Johnny's torch on the table in the other room. He fetched this, and clutching the hammer descended the steps into the cellar.

'Whoever this is, I'm going to find them,' he muttered to himself. 'The others—they meant nothing to me. Nick meant everything. I *loved* him...'

For several minutes, he explored the labyrinth of dirty, dingy passages, keeping his back to the wall while training the beam of the spotlight in every nook and cranny. In one compartment, he discovered a pile of coal—not the one they had been filling their buckets from. Then his foot struck against something soft.

'God almighty...'

Using the toe of his shoe, he kicked away a few pieces of coal, and then he saw it.

A hand...

Setting down the hammer, Trevor knelt down and used both hands to move the coal. He recognised at once the dark material of Jack Gibbons' donkey jacket. Then, out of the corner of his eye he observed a darkened shape behind him—and another hand, reaching for the hammer.

8: Denouement

Mike Brent climbed up the ladder, hoisted his hefty frame through the open window, and noiselessly dropped to the floor on the other side.

'I'd make a bloody good burglar,' he mused to himself. 'And I need my head read for coming back here. If Johnny had come with me to look for the phone like he wanted to, we'd have been miles away by now...'

He went into the bedroom. Johnny was not there, so he descended the stairs. His lover was not in the other room, either—nobody was. He started to panic.

'Johnny? Nick...Trevor?'

There was no response, so he checked the other downstairs rooms—the scullery last of all. The cellar door was open, and scattered across the floor in front of were pieces of broken crockery, and beyond this what appeared to be a pool of blood. He stooped to examine this, and was about to dip his finger into the gooey mess when he observed the light coming from the bottom of the steps—Johnny's flashlight, obviously where he had dropped it on the dusty floor.

'Shit...'

His heart thumping, and both fists clenched, Mike descended the steps, picked up the torch and shone it about him. Moments later he found Trevor, spread-eagled on his front, across the coal. He managed to turn him over, and his face was almost unrecognisable. And underneath Trevor's body, that of Jack Gibbons, the driver of the minibus.

'Mother of God,' he muttered. 'Johnny...'

137

He charged back up the steps, screaming his lover's name. Just as he reached the top, the cellar door slammed into his face, and everything went black.

Nick Quinn stood, grinning sheepishly, in the middle of the room. He was wearing Trevor's sweater—the one he had loaned him earlier, and nervously threaded his fingers through his thick, dark hair.

Mike was aware that he was sitting down, but initially conscious of nothing else other than that his head was spinning like a top. The pain, when he finally opened his eyes, was more agonising than anything he had ever felt before, but soon disappeared once he became aware of his surroundings. He tried to move, but was unable to. His wrists were bound, and his feet were tied to the legs of one of the dining chairs.

'It wasn't the nurse at all,' he blurted out. 'It was you! And now it's my turn...'

Nick crossed the room. He was swinging a length of rope. Mike swallowed hard and Nick laughed—not the nervous, boyish laugh Mike had often heard while they had been holed up in this house, but an evil, deep-throated growl. Even Nick's eyes had changed. Yesterday, Johnny had remarked how sexy he found these. Now they were cold and calculating, bringing with inexplicable hatred.

'No, Mike. I'm not going to strangle you. I've already used that one—Janet, remember? Nope, I've got a cosy little number lined up for you, and for Johnny-Boy, as you lovingly like to call him...'

'Johnny,' Mike got out. 'What have you done with him?'

Nick giggled, and flung the rope aside. 'I haven't *done* anything with him—*yet*! He's sleeping peacefully at the moment, in the bogey-room with the others. I found a little something in Janet's bag—nothing too harsh, just a gentle little sedative. The one she was doling out to dotty Kate—I just doubled the dose. Ha, that almost sounds poetic! I'm leaving Johnny-Boy until last. Once I've done away with you, I'm going to have him. Your boyfriend's going to die with one hell of a smile on his face...'

'Cunt,' Mike spat out.

Nick knelt at his victim's feet, and checked the knots in the rope which secured him to the chair.

'Best to be safe rather than sorry,' he mused.

He stood up, unzipped his trousers, and pulled out his thick, hard cock.

'See this?' he grinned, working the foreskin back and forth. 'It's been stiff as a steel rod for hours. Trevor was practically begging for it, less than an hour ago. Had to blow him—such a cute cock. I got him so turned on that he blew his muck almost at once. I could have you, right now if I wanted, and I'd still be hard and ready to pop another load when it's Johnny-Boy's turn. I even thought about it—about taking you from behind, and slitting your gizzard at the very zenith of our passion. But I've used that one, too. And cute as you may be, you're the last man in the world I'd want to fuck, Mike. The *last* man...'

Mike struggled to free himself, aware that he probably

was wasting his time, though the ropes around his ankles appeared to give *just* a little.

'Won't be long, now,' Nick scoffed, pushing his cock back inside his trousers, and licking his fingers.

'You're fucking nuts,' Mike growled. 'All this time we've been blaming an innocent woman...'

'And I suppose you'll be wanting to know *why* I did it,' the other put in. 'I guess I owe you that much before I send you on your way—before I go back upstairs and fuck that gorgeous boyfriend of yours to hell and back, before sending him to heaven?'

'What have you done to him, you vile shit?' Mike growled, and this time when he struggled, the ropes *did* slacken a tad.

Nick chuckled. 'Like I said, I just gave him a little something to make him sleep. Don't worry, I'm not going to hurt him until I've had my wicked, wicked way with him. I want to make *him* come too. Don't ever let it be said that Nick Quinn was an inconsiderate lover. Then the two of you will be together—for eternity!'

Mike only wished that he might break free of the much tighter bonds which secured his wrists, so that he might grab hold of this psychopath and snap his neck.

'Why Johnny?' he asked. 'Why *any* of us? What have we ever done to *you*?'

'Oh,' he returned. '*You've* done plenty. I've had this planned for a long time, my friend. Six months or more. The problem was, when and where. Believe me, it's not easy trying to bump someone off in the middle of a fucking

140

great metropolis! So I had to think of an alternative. I must admit, you've given me quite a headache these past few months. I've spent many a sleepless night wondering how I would do it—how I would get away with it. Then fate came to my rescue, you might say. I found myself here, in this old house. I killed six people, Mike—and all because of you!'

'I didn't even know these people until a few days ago,' Mike began. 'You're bluffing. Why would you want to do that? It was the nurse...'

He had started to perspire. Sweat trickled down the back of his neck and coursed between his shoulder-blades. The palms of his hands were sticky—itching to get at this man and rip him apart.

'I know *everything* about you,' Nick went on. 'Ha, I might even know a few things about you that you don't even know about yourself. Thirty-seven. Former rugger player—booted out of your team for sexually assaulting another player. Well, actually you gave his cock a playful tug, probably hoping that it would lead to better things, but the guy took it the wrong way and made a big deal about it. Ten-Inch Brent. That's what they called you! And Johnny Rodrigues, the celebrated crime writer—been your squeeze for what, ten years now? You've travelled the world together, searching for exotic locations for his pathetic little stories, only this time he wanted his characters to be slumming it in a caravan park—or was it a camping site, in the middle of Dartmoor? Normally you would have driven down here, but you've both had your licenses revoked...'

'How the fuck do you *know* all this?' Mike demanded. 'Who *are* you, for Christ's sake?'

'Oh,' he replied, the Elvis grin suddenly turning sardonic. 'I *know*, all right. I was standing right behind you when you booked your seats for the train. You even made it easier for me by telling the guy behind the ticket desk exactly where you were heading—some place I'd never heard of, smack in the middle of the moors. You asked for the quiet coach—cracked a little joke about B standing for Brent—so I did likewise. I wanted to study you a little more before doing the deed. Then I went home and checked it all out on the Internet. You were going to be staying at a little site out in the middle of nowhere—perfect! I'd follow you, hide out until you were asleep and just pray the weather stayed fine—then, bang! I've seen some of those caravan windows, little more than thick sheets of plastic. The bullets would have zipped through, no problem at all, straight into your thick Irish skull. And of course, Johnny-Boy would have had to die too. I couldn't afford to leave any witnesses behind, could I? He would know that better than anyone, crime being his trade, so to speak.'

Mike swallowed hard, as once again Nick unzipped his trousers. Shoving one hand inside, he began toying with his cock, then grinned even more sardonically than before.

'Would you like to blow me, Mike?' he asked. 'You know, before I send you on your way?'

Mike found himself nodding, and he was thinking to himself, 'I'll *blow* you all right, you deranged bastard. Just shove your dick in my mouth and I'll bite the fucking end off it, and you'll bleed to death…'

Maybe Nick was reading his mind as he zipped his trousers up again and shoved his hand in his pocket.

'No,' he grinned. 'Maybe *this* is a weapon more suited to the occasion!'

He fished out a tiny pistol. and Mike all but heaved.

'Oh, before you ask—yes, it's real,' he sneered. '*And* it's loaded. I guess you could say *both* of my weapons are loaded. It should have been just you and Johnny-Boy, but it snowed and we ended up here. I had to put my thinking-cap on about that—decided to play a little game with you all. I mean, if I was risking carrying the can for killing two, why not have a little fun and bump off the lot of you?'

'Even Trevor?' Mike spat back. 'You conned that poor kid into thinking you were in love with him, you bastard!'

'Great fuck, though,' he returned. 'The truth is, I *was* in love with him—passionately, *madly* in love with him. I've never been one for making off the cuff decisions, but the minute I set eyes on Trevor, I knew he was the one. Trevor touched parts of me I never knew I had. Somehow I don't think Johnny-Boy's going to be quite as good. He won't be nice and tight like I prefer them—not after he's had that ugly fat schlong of yours inside him. But in his own way, Trevor was happy to die. His world had suddenly collapsed about his ears because he'd just found my body on the kitchen floor. Ah, the wonders of tomato soup!'

Nick circled around him, pausing every now and then to poke him in the ribs with the nozzle of the gun. Mike had

143

seen a few guns in his time, while accompanying Johnny on his visits to various forensic labs, and he was almost certain that this one was a fake—but he did not wish to push him too far, just in case he was mistaken. And those ropes around his ankles had slackened some more...

'I killed the driver first,' Nick explained. 'You all suspected poor old Jack Gibbons—that was his name—yet he was the first for the chop. Well, an iron bar to be exact, the one Trevor had down the side of the bed in case the bogey man wandered into the room in the middle of the night. You see, Gibbons knew where we were—like the back of his hand, he said. I didn't want him calling the cops. His was the only mobile I couldn't get to and remove the SIM card. Well, Colonel Tom and Mrs Moppet didn't have one. So I followed him down the cellar and clobbered him—buried him under one of the piles of coal. I knew none of you lot would have the guts to go down there. Then I killed the colonel—surly old git. I saw the nurse with the scalpel—she used it for your knee. I caught him outside your room, watching you through a crack in the door and having a sly wank. Blew his wad all down the door-frame. That gave me an idea...'

'Can't wait to hear it,' Mike gruffed.

Each time Nick Quinn turned his back on him, albeit for a few seconds, Mike coughed and shuffled in the chair, and the ropes slackened just that little bit more.

'The colonel was sitting on the pan,' Nick went on. 'I pretended I was feeling rough—told him I was going to throw up. The sink's right next to the toilet. I leaned over it,

144

then reached across and stuck the scalpel in his neck, hammered it home with the heel of my shoe. That was a few minutes before I went with Dave to look for the phone box—gave us an alibi, of sorts. Then we found the bungalow. *That* was fun! After I'd disconnected all the phones I talked Dave into having a little fun, too. Great fuck —still not as good as Trevor, though. Then I caught *them* at it—Trevor and Dave, on the bloody landing of all places, until they had the sense to go into one of the bedrooms. Trevor thought I was asleep. Then when he came back and he thought *I* was asleep, I collared Dave. He'd come back upstairs, so I showed him my little metal friend here—forced him back into the bedroom and made him lie on the floor. Slit his throat with my Army knife, the one that used to belong to Mark...'

Nick grabbed the back of one of the armchairs, swung it so that it was facing Mike, and slumped into it.

'I really did think I'd found a replacement for Mark, with Trevor. He was sitting opposite me on the train. We clicked at once—even had a little fun in the toilet. I actually told him that I *loved* him. We could have had a future together. Then I saw him cheating on me with Dave. In all our years together, Mark and I never so much as looked at another man. If any love affair was perfect, ours was...'

Mike remembered what he had seen at the bungalow.

'You cheated on Trevor first' he gruffed. 'I saw the johnnies in the ashtray.'

'With Dave it was mechanical, a spur of the moment thing,' he responded coldly. 'No emotion was involved. The

145

excitement of breaking into the place—our nerves were all jangled and we needed to release a little pressure. I stood in the shadows and watched Trevor and Dave on the landing, then I watched through the key-hole while they were in the other room. That was no spur-of-the-moment thing. They'd planned it. There was every danger that Dave would have taken Trevor away from me. I'd already lost one lover...'

'Better to kill him that let someone else have him,' Mike began. 'Very noble of you...'

Nick did not reply to this. He said, 'The old biddy was the easiest. I'd found the poison on a shelf in the cellar when I buried Gibbons under the coal. Then there was the nurse and her bloody diary. I was sure she was on to me, so I nicked it. God, that woman had problems! They found her last patient at the bottom of the stairs with a broken neck, and suspected she'd done it to get the money. Turned out she wasn't there when it happened. But the other things she'd gotten up to. And she *was* on to me. She wrote in her diary how she'd seen me coming out of the bathroom—minutes before Dave and I went looking for the phone. She didn't actually write that I'd killed the colonel, only that no one had used the bathroom between me using it and Johnny finding him, which amounted to the same thing. So I sneaked upstairs after you came back down—strangled her in the bath. She'd made it easier by lying in the tub the wrong way round—I guess she wanted to keep her eye on the door, so I fastened the scarf around the taps to make you all think she'd topped herself. Nurse Ellis, couldn't cope with her guilt any longer….Mind you, I

146

almost botched the whole thing up. The bitch came at me with a pair of scissors...'

He raised the bottom of his sweater, then his T-shirt. Mike observed, partially hidden by the dense black bristles, a tiny fresh cut to the right of his navel.

'But as they say, every cloud has a silver lining,' he went on. 'After I'd dispatched her, I closed the door and wedged the scissors under the bottom...'

Nick leered as he said this. Dipping into his pocket, he produced the bright red Swiss Army knife he had mentioned a few minutes ago, and opened its largest blade, still encrusted with Dave Rose's blood. Mike held his breath as Nick got up out of the armchair and slowly advanced towards him.

'This was in Mark's pocket, the day he died,' he said. 'The police came around to the flat and gave me his things—all neatly labeled and stuffed into a big plastic bag. That's all that his life finally amounted to. A big plastic bag, and a corpse on a mortuary slab...'

He grabbed the front of Mike's sweater, forcing his head back. Under this, he was wearing a T-shirt and an athletic vest. Nick pushed the blade of the knife through the material, and Mike winced as the point pricked his flesh. He closed his eyes and awaited the end. He had never been a religious man, but he prayed right now—not for himself, but for Johnny, who was to be this maniac's next victim.

Nick worked the blade downwards towards Mike's waist, slicing through the several layers of clothing, and exposing his heaving chest and abs. Mike was sure that he

147

was going to throw up, but after a moment the feeling of nausea passed.

'You think you're going to get away with this, don't you?' he began. 'Right now the cops are on their way...'

Nick Quinn chuckled at this. Leaning forwards, he tweaked a nipple. 'You obviously think that I came down with the last shower. The police know absolutely nothing about this place, unless of course you've informed them by carrier pigeon. I've already told you how I disabled everyone's cell phones—how I clipped all the cables in the bungalow. This morning, after disabling Johnny-Boy, so to speak, and bidding a sad farewell to Trevor, I followed you. There's another way of getting to the telephone box. You'd have known that if you'd studied Johnny's map—oops, that suddenly went missing, just like Janet's diary! And how stranger that *that* ended up in Johnny's rucksack! It's still there, by the way. I put it back while you were out, along with the pages I ripped out which will have Johnny's prints all over them. But I digress. There's a path across a field that cuts a good five minutes off the trek. Trevor had told me on the train that he was coming down here to spend the long Easter weekend with his boyfriend. I saw the way he kept looking every time someone mentioned the phone box, so when I saw him climbing out of the window I'd an idea where he was going, so I sneaked out and followed him. I don't think the others even noticed I was gone. You and Johnny were otherwise engaged—fucking, I don't doubt. I got there before him—cut the wire, and hid by the edge. Trevor must have had second thoughts….He turned around before he got to the phone box and started to make his way back here. I beat him to it! Remember how they found the colonel with his cock in his hand? Well, when they finally see what's happened here—I guess that'll be the next time a potential punter comes to view the place—they'll find eight corpses, in varying states of decay. And sitting in that chair, with his wrists slit and the knife on the floor beside him, will be the guy who did it all before taking the easy way out. I'll be sitting at home—watching it on the news, and Mark will have been well and truly avenged...'

'Mark,' Mike shot back. 'Who the fuck is this Mark who you keep rabbiting on about? And what does he have to do with me—with Johnny?'

Nick's eyes suddenly welled with tears.

'You really haven't cottoned on yet, have you? Mark Anthony Neville. Does that name ring any bells?'

Mike started.

Had he really said *Mark Anthony Neville*?

'That's right,' Nick went on. 'Mark and I were going to be married. Our families had supported us right from the very start. The ceremony had been booked—the reception paid for. Then, with just two weeks to go, some fucking drunken driver forced him off the road. Mark didn't stand a chance. And you—you murdering Irish shit—you got off with a fine and a suspended sentence!'

'But it was an accident,' Mike began. 'It wasn't even me driving...'

Nick was not listening. He wiped his eyes on his jacket cuff—and did not see the foot which took advantage

149

of this lapse of concentration, which suddenly came up and kicked him so hard in the nuts that he screamed and the knife flew out of his hand. Then there was another sound, coming from somewhere behind him. Mike saw something silver and shiny come whizzing through the air—saw Nick Quinn hit the deck, before he himself passed out.

It was over.

Epilogue

The room was large and extremely well-appointed, possessed of every luxury—what they had come to expect of a five-star hotel. Since coming here, in the wake of their ordeal, they had not once set foot out of the door. When they had needed fresh air, they had relaxed on the heated balcony, gazing out across the beach, well clear of the still foul weather.

This morning, the police had called. Nick Quinn had been found dead in his cell, less than twelve hours after being charged on seven counts of murder. The sergeant had but scant details, and neither Mike nor Johnny had felt the slightest twinge of regret.

'It's the sort of thing that shouldn't happen,' Johnny had told him. 'The police make every effort to ensure the prisoner won't top himself, but if that's their intention then there's no stopping them. They'll bang their heads against the wall until their brains fall out—they'll bite through the veins in their wrists. Good riddance to bad rubbish is about all I can say.'

Quinn had killed them all in cold blood—all because he had been wanting to get at the one man he had believed to be responsible for the death of his lover, Mark Anthony Neville.

The whole messy affair had made the front pages of most of the nationals, and certain facts—not mentioned at the time of Mark Anthony Neville's death—had emerged. Mike Brent had *not* been at the wheel of the car at the time of the accident. Johnny Rodrigues had—and after swerving to avoid the vehicle speeding towards them on the wrong side of the road, Johnny had slammed on the brakes and watched, through his rear-view mirror, as it had slammed into a tree, instantly killing its occupant. Within minutes, the police had arrived at the scene, and Mike had lied to them that *he* had been driving—taking the rap because Johnny had been in the middle of a four months ban after being caught doing forty in a thirty zone when he had been in a hurry to get a friend to the station. The police had breathalised Mike. He had subsequently been fined and given a ban, but only on account of the drink-driving charge. He had been exonerated completely of causing the other car to crash—Mark Anthony Neville was later found to have been three times over the legal limit, and several witnesses had only minutes earlier swerved to avoid him hitting them. Nick Quinn had been informed of this, but such had been his distress over losing his lover that he had lost all sense of reason. Had he not taken his own life, the sergeant told Mike and Johnny, he would have spent the rest of his life in prison—maybe Broadmoor—without any hope of parole.

At the old house, while Mike had been out looking for the phone box, Quinn had cornered Johnny on the landing—pulling the gun, he had smacked him across the back of the head, stunning him long enough to administer the two phials he had found in Janet Ellis' medicine bag. The police had found the gun, and it had not been a fake. Dragging Johnny into the room containing the corpses of some of his other victims, Quinn had left him there with the intent of killing him later—but only after forcing him to have sex with him. Johnny had pretended to be losing consciousness, and the moment Quinn had left the room he had shoved his fingers down his throat and brought back the sedative. Removing his shoes, he had crept downstairs and stood outside the door—not just listening to Quinn's confession, but recording it on the killer's mobile, which he had left next to his bed—confident that when he returned to collect it, the last of his victims would have been dead. And at the exact moment that Mike had booted him in the balls, Johnny had flung the cast-iron pan at him which he had picked up in the scullery—a perfect shot which had hit him smack between the eyes, knocking him out cold.

Now, their ordeal was over and they lay naked on the bed, more in love than ever before—if such a thing was possible. Last night, after spending four hours at the police station, they had been so exhausted they had fallen asleep with their clothes on, clothes which bore the odour of blood and death. This morning, before their shower, they had shoved them into a rubbish bag provided by the hotel.

Mike chuckled himself. Leaning his head against Johnny's shoulder, he toyed with the strong black hairs between his lover's pecs.

'God,' Johnny murmured. 'I'm going to be having nightmares about that fucking place for the rest of my life.'

Mike could only chuckle at this.

'Me too,' he said.

'Then what's so amusing about it all?' Johnny asked. 'You don't see *me* laughing...'

'It's you, Johnny-Boy,' he grinned. 'In all the years that I've known you—it'll be eleven years next month—that's the first time I've *ever* heard you swear!'

Johnny smiled, ruefully. 'Well, I guess there's a first time for everything. It's the first time I've been close to you in almost a week when you haven't smelled like a dustbin!'

He snuggled that little bit closer, and slung one arm across his lover's smooth, muscular chest. In his estimation, Mike had never looked lovelier—a beautiful, gentle giant.His long fair hair, spread across the satin pillow, shone like spun gold. His steely eyes were like sapphires, mischievous but impeccably honest. Yesterday, in that house, Johnny had been truly terrified while waiting for the precise moment to bring Nick Quinn down—had push come to shove, he would have taken a bullet to save his Mike's life—this was how much he loved him. But now, they were safe.

Johnny's hand descended slowly, caressing the washboard abs, tugging at the little hairs here before running his fingers through the fluffy, honey-blond pubes.

'It's also the first time in almost a week that I've seen what your cock looks like in the daylight,' he mused. 'Is it just my eyes, or has being in the shade for so long made it grow an extra inch—you now, like when they stick a bucket over rhubarb?'

Wrapping his long fingers around his favourite weapon, Johnny felt it stiffen in his hand as he gently drew back the fleshy foreskin—'Ten-Inch Brent', returned to normality. Johnny was hard too, solid as a rock, his slightly

154

smaller but less wrist-thick cock pressed against Mike's thigh. Moving further down the bed, he aimed straight for the jackpot—the big, vee-shaped purple head with its wet, smiling slit. But before opening wide Johnny rotated his body 180 degrees, rewarding Mike with a faceful of warm, hairy scrotum and a perfect view of his densely-forested anal Valhalla.

For a good twenty minutes, their lips and tongues explored each other's nether regions—Mike lapping the hard ridge between nutsack and butt-hole, then bending Johnny's cock back between his thighs, and swallowing the meaty-tasting head and a good half of the rope-veined shaft, drawing his knees up to his chest so that Johnny could thumb his buns apart and pig out on his sphincter which had never tasted *this* good while they had been incarcerated in the old house.

Eventually, they came up for air, and lay side by side for a moment gazing into one another's eyes, trying not to relive their dreadful experiences of the last few days, or thinking about what might have happened—until Johnny snapped them out of it by reaching for the lube.

'It won't last long,' he breathed. 'We're way too excited...'

Mike spread his massive rugger player's thighs and touched his chest with his knees. Johnny eased himself between them, delivering little butterfly kisses to each side of Mike's throat. Then, staring hard into his eyes once more, he reached down with one hand and very slowly guided his cock inside him.

155

'That feels so good, Johnny-Boy...'

For a few minutes, Johnny did not move at all. Leaning forwards, he kissed each nipple tenderly, turning it into an ebony knob. Then he brushed his lips against Mike's left shoulder, and traced them along his collarbone to the hollow in his throat, followed the stubble upwards to his chin, and eventually his mouth. Mike repositioned his knees, hooking the backs of them on either side of Johnny's neck, an action which saw Johnny feeding him all eight inches of cock, until his pubes dug into his sphincter and his nuts slapped against his tailbone, heavy with their two-day load.

'Fuck me, Johnny-Boy. Fuck me hard. I don't care if it lasts half an hour or half a minute. We've got all the time in the world, and a hell of a lot to catch up on...'

Clasping his big, shovel-like hands over the dimpled cheeks of Johnny's arse, he dug the tips of his fingers deep into the hairy channel and Johnny groaned his appreciation. It certainly had not been as vigorous as this in the old house, otherwise the clapped-out bed there would have collapsed under the strain and they might have ended up plummeting through the floor and into the room below! Gripping the melon biceps for support, Johnny gave him his all like he always had. At last, things were back to normal!

They rutted like wild animals until the very last second when, summoning his full strength, Johnny dragged his cock free to spray the full velocity of his load across the man beneath him...a half dozen copious spurts which jetted across Mike's torso like white hot darts. Mike was gritting his teeth and about to let go, but Johnny made his climax that much more powerful and brought about a lion's roar by slamming back into him, just as the first ripper shot upwards and crashed against his chest, followed by several more which frosted the black, sweat-drenched carpet which covered most of his torso.

It took them a while to return to the land of the living, and when they finally rolled onto their backs, panting for breath and their chests and abs streaked with the produce of their passion—their cocks still semi-hard and both well aware that their balls were by no means empty, that they really *did* have a lot of catching up to do—Mike placed a tiny, velvet-covered box on Johnny's stomach.

'I've been thinking about this for some time,' he said. 'Really, we should have done this years ago...'

Johnny opened the box, and the broad smile lit up his handsome face—but still he could not resist a tear.

'The answer's yes,' he replied, as Mike slipped the ring on to his finger.

.

Printed in Great Britain
by Amazon

80899215R00092